TRAPPED!

DONALIE BELTRAN

TRAPPED!

ISBN-10: 0-9896362-4-0
ISBN-13:978-0-9896362-4-7

Available in paperback and ebook

Editor: Frank Kresen

Published by: Killing Time Press, LLC

DEDICATION

This book is dedicated to my loving father, Raymond Lee Tuxhorn, who passed away while I was writing this story. I know he would have enjoyed reading it, and is probably doing so in Heaven.

I love and miss you so much, Dad. We'll all be together again before you know it.

CONTENTS

ACKNOWLEDGMENTS

I would like to thank my beta readers, great authors in their own right, Walter Danley and Mike Boggia. Through them I learned what I had done right and what was wrong. Thank you, my friends, for your time and support.

I also need to acknowledge what is not real in this story. I pride myself in making sure my stories are well researched so the reader is in the real world. However, after a call to the Dallas FBI, I decided it would be 'prudent' to alter the description of the main post office.

The obvious reason is because some disturbed individual may try to duplicate this tragedy. Please understand I had planned to become very familiar with this facility, but because of this decision, I never visited this post office and all descriptions of the interior are fiction.

CHAPTER

ONE

Fire is everywhere! Run, run for shelter! Everyone is screaming! He was running for his life through the woods, and he didn't even know why. Children crying and screaming for help. Bombs going off. He did his best to get out of harm's way. The terror was so real he couldn't remember where he was or why he was there.

What happened? A loud explosion turned the world around him to black.

Ears still ringing, the only thing he could see is the flames. He turned in circles with his rifle ready, but he didn't know who to shoot. He tried to get behind a tree for cover when someone yelled, "LOOK OUT!" He looked up to see a child holding a grenade. That's when he knew he was going to die.

With a scream, twenty-eight year old ex-Marine Sergeant-Major Tag Reynolds woke from his nightmare. Nightmares were not unusual these days. When he realized he was safe at home, Tag lay his pounding head back down on the bathroom floor and passed out again.

~~~

Grace Reynolds awoke frightened by some loud noise that made her sit straight up in bed. *Did someone scream?* The clock showed it was almost time to get up. An internal kick in the ribs from her unborn child also told her to get out of bed.

Nine months pregnant, Grace was sure her baby wasn't any happier than she with that terrifying scream. Her heart still pounding wildly, she knew the baby also felt her fear. Grace did a slow-breathing exercise as she stood on her feet. With some effort, maybe the baby would settle down. Maybe they both would settle down. It took about five minutes, but she managed to breathe easy, and she could tell her child was resting.

She waddled her way to the bathroom and stopped when she spotted her husband, Tag, lying on the floor beside the toilet. She was pretty sure the scream had come from him, but he had passed out again. This had become commonplace. The room stunk of vomit and alcohol.

Because of this continuing behavior, she'd made a point of cleaning the bathroom every night so she could take a shower and get ready for bed. Grace knew that, by morning, the room would be gross again. She was ashamed to think this lifestyle had become 'normal' to her. To them both.

After cleaning the sink, she brushed her teeth and washed her face. Before leaving the room, she once again glanced down at her six-foot-two husband, who hadn't moved since she'd come in. His name, Tag, was Irish and meant 'handsome.'

No doubt about it: My husband fits the name, but I'd bet if his parents looked down on him today, they might not think so!

Grace immediately regretted her thoughts, as Tag had lost his parents when he was in college. Grace was twenty-five years old and still had her parents. Even though they had disowned her several years ago, at least they were still alive.

Tag was a war veteran who'd returned from his second tour a little more than ten months ago. Returning to civilian life was his preference after going through several months of PTSD therapy in the military.

He told her they had been treated like losers. Soldiers were treated like they *pretended* to have a problem so they could get out of work. Tag was outraged and opted to remove himself from those hypocrites.

They fought for our country only to be thrown away like traitors! She remembered how angry he'd been for several weeks after leaving the Marines, and Grace could hardly blame him. *Treatment of our troops returning from war is disgraceful.*

The Dallas newspaper had run an exposé on how badly the returning troops were being treated. No one could believe the government could get away with such despicable treatment of their own soldiers, when they constantly told the media they were helping. *Yeah, right!*

After his anger had subsided, being a civilian again was not too bad for the first couple of months, but things started to change. Not being able to find employment produced one of the first problems for Tag. That resulted in self-pity and then anger at Grace for having to support them.

She couldn't believe it: He was angry with *her* for bringing in a paycheck! As a well-known columnist for a national fashion magazine, if it hadn't been for her decent pay, they would have been on the street. Literally. Tag didn't seem to think of that when he complained about her working.

It wasn't long after that when he told her he had been having horrible nightmares for some time, making him think he was back in the war zone. Grace assumed his trying to get a handle on those nightmares was what had led to the drinking. But, she wasn't even trying to figure it out anymore.

Grace knew a little about PTSD — at least what the media made of it. It's apparently not uncommon among returning soldiers, so it wasn't hard to find support groups outside the military. Tag said they didn't understand 'his' problem, and so he stopped going to meetings. *So,* what was *'his'* problem? Why was *'his'* so different from everyone else's? She just didn't understand it any more. The war had taken away her husband, and she didn't know how to get him back.

He didn't even try to find a job any more. Tag had not been on an interview in months. She didn't care if he washed windows, as long as he had something to fill his time besides drinking. This past month, he'd slept more nights on the bathroom floor than he had in their own bed. Alcohol was apparently his comfort of choice.

Grace loved him with all her heart — there was no denying that. She had even been disowned by her parents for marrying him. But if things didn't change once the baby came, she didn't know if their relationship could survive. Raising a child in this atmosphere wasn't an option. She would still love him, but she wouldn't live with a drunk.

Back in her bedroom, she put on the only decent maternity outfit she had left that fit, a red sundress. Because it was one of her favorites, she wanted to have it cut down after the baby came so she could continue to wear it. The red complemented her long, wavy black hair.

Grace had heard how some women couldn't wait for their nine months of 'misery' to be over, but she had enjoyed every minute. The end of her pregnancy would be an even-greater blessing, by having the baby to hold instead of carrying him inside.

Grateful for her sit-down vanity table in the bedroom, she'd made a point of putting on her makeup and fixing her hair every day. Her long hair was easy to keep, as it flowed about her face and down her back with soft, shiny waves. Sometimes she wore it up, but today Grace let it fall. Then she put considerable effort into making her face look perfect.

After she'd applied makeup to her fair skin, lined her brown eyes in black, and applied mascara to her long lashes, she added blush and a pale lipstick to complete the picture.

She'd gone on paid maternity leave just a couple of days before, with the baby due in a week. Unlike many other mothers-to-be, to Grace, having to spend time at home didn't mean she would let herself go. She would never allow that to happen. Every day she made sure to pull herself together, just like she would if she were going to work.

Satisfied with her reflection in the mirror, she carefully made her way down the stairs. She and Tag had initially talked about getting a single-level, two-bedroom apartment before the baby came, but now she doubted that Tag even remembered the conversation, let alone cared. They couldn't afford it on her one paycheck anyway. The Dallas area was not the cheapest place to live, but they both loved living here and wanted to make it work.

Today she planned to get all the used baby clothes she had collected washed and put away. If she had time, she wanted to get at least some of the baby furniture put together.

Would she be able to do it alone? Holding those pieces together would not be easy, especially if she had to get down on the floor. *Tag would be too busy with his next bottle to help.* She was angry thinking about it. Never had Grace believed her strong — and yes, *handsome* — husband would become a drunk.

Reaching the kitchen, she decided on a cup of decaf and a piece of toast. When Baby Reynolds gave a kick, Grace took it as a sign that he, too, was hungry, so she added another piece of toast to the menu. She rubbed her stomach as her coffee maker brewed her drink and the toaster worked on the bread.

While waiting, Grace looked out the kitchen window. The day was another beautiful April morning in Dallas. She opened the window to let in the fresh air. The soft, cool breeze quickly picked up her spirits. Spring always did that to her.

As parents, they didn't want to know the sex of their baby in advance, so they requested not to be told. But she always felt he was a boy and used the masculine pronouns when talking about him. Grace couldn't wait for him to arrive. She'd never thought she could feel this way, but from the moment she saw the positive home pregnancy test, she had loved the child growing inside of her.

Male names came to her all the time, and she would pick a favorite. But that would last only until another name hit her and she loved it more. Today, the reigning name was Striker Jon Reynolds.

She laughed out loud as she thought of it again. *Hey, it appeals to me!* She never had to worry about input from Tag. He didn't care what they named their son. He didn't even care about his son.

The first few weeks of her pregnancy, he'd felt the same excitement about the baby as she did. *Now he doesn't think about anything but himself.* That knowledge brought her spirits back down.

After putting a small amount of butter on the toast and a teaspoon of sugar in her coffee cup, she took her plate into the dining room. This had become the room where everything happened, including the sacks of baby clothes she needed to take care of. She moved some paperwork to the side to find a place to put her plate down on the table.

That's when she saw it.

CHAPTER

TWO

When she looked closer at the envelope, she realized it was their income taxes. Their taxes...which Tag was supposed to have mailed *last* week! Worse yet, *today* was tax day — the 15th!

"TAG NELSON REYNOLDS!" she yelled toward the ceiling while gritting her teeth. "You forgot to mail our taxes, and they have to be in the mail *TODAY!*"

The sound of movement came from upstairs and then some shuffling. *Gee, does that mean macho man is off the bathroom floor?*

"What should we do?" She yelled up at him again.

"Take them down to the main post office. That way, they will get postmarked today," Tag's muffled voice sounded a mile away. She heard what sounded like their bedroom door close.

Grace looked down at the papers and then back at the ceiling.

Really? Really, Tag? Nine months pregnant; can no longer drive; and I have to be the one heading into downtown Dallas to get the envelope postmarked, when you should have mailed them days ago? REALLY?

She wanted to go upstairs and give him a piece of her mind but didn't want to tackle those stairs again. When she got home this afternoon, he would be up and, hopefully, not too drunk by then. That's when they would talk.

Boy, are we going to talk! This crap is going to stop, or I am out of here! One baby is all I can take care of at a time!

She was angry when she sat down to drink her coffee and put a little something in her stomach. So mad at her husband, Grace almost didn't hear the knock on the door.

Getting up slowly and making her way to the door, she was not surprised to see it was Jerry Barker. He had been Tag's best friend since grade school and had also served with him in the Marines. Now he was dear to both of them.

"Hey, Jer," Grace smiled. She tried to give him a hug which was difficult to do around a large stomach. They both laughed after the clumsy effort.

Always glad to see him, she said, "If you are looking for Tag, he is passed out upstairs. I think he's in the bedroom now. And before you ask, yes, he started out at his favorite place, in the bathroom, hugging the toilet."

"Aw, Grace, I'm sorry."

"Not your fault, Jer. It's all on him. Come on in, and I will make you a cup of coffee." Her spirits picked back up to see the man who always seemed to be there for her and Tag. She couldn't imagine him not being in their lives.

"You look gorgeous, as usual. Don't know how Tag got so lucky as to catch a beauty like you."

Both were grinning at the familiar joking when Jerry went on, "Before I sit down, I want to go up and check on

Tag, if you don't mind." Jerry always cared about Tag and his recovery.

Grace thought, *Lucky will be the woman who finally captures his love.* She nodded toward the stairs and headed back to the kitchen for more coffee. Jerry took the steps two at a time, getting to the top. She heard the bedroom door open, but nothing else. It only took a moment for Jerry to come back down.

"Tag's asleep, on the bed this time. I just like to check and make sure he's still breathing." Seeing the sorrow on Jerry's face, Grace understood only too well.

He sat down in the dining room with his cup of coffee while Grace went back to her own cup and the toast.

"Jer, I just don't know if Tag and I can make it if something doesn't change. I can't have a baby growing up around this." She pointed toward the ceiling.

"I know, and I don't blame you a bit, pretty lady, but don't do anything too quickly. I still have faith in Tag."

That was Jerry. Always there to support his friend.

"You have to understand, post-traumatic stress disorder is not easy to get over. I know you get tired of hearing about it, and I imagine most spouses do, but it is very real, and, Grace, Tag *is* suffering."

"I know. I *do*. But how long before it goes away? How long before my husband comes back to me? What in the world can I do to make that happen?"

Jerry thought for a moment before speaking, "You have to be patient. The man you married is not the man who came home from overseas. He is hurt, insecure, and angry at all the horrible things he saw there. Like all of us, he felt helpless to stop it. We saw women and children blown apart, for no reason! Things like that can really do a number on you."

"But, what about you? You haven't turned to the bottle. How did you escape it all?"

Again Jerry thought a while before speaking. "My personality is different from Tag's. He is the serious one, and that makes all these things hit him harder. My whole life, I have been able to laugh off my problems, at least most of them. Sort of walk away from my troubles, I guess.

"I have been blessed, I know. But, then again, Grace, there is a lot you don't see about me. No, I haven't turned to drinking, but I do have nightmares.

Loud noises make me jump sky high!" Jerry smiled at that one.

"But I have been more fortunate than Tag in other ways, too. When I came home, I had a Mom and Dad ready to care for me. I immediately went back to work in Dad's construction company, which gives me the ability to take off when I need to be in class or study — *or* just can't handle the depression that day. If you remember, Dad offered Tag a job, too, but he wasn't ready yet. Now, Tag wouldn't be able to put in a day's work at any job."

Jerry wanted to get his degree in business so he could take over when his Dad decided to retire. He had only four months left before he graduated. Grace couldn't have been more proud of him. Tag already had his degree and, at one time, she thought Tag and Jerry would make quite the pair working together. *That, obviously, won't happen!*

"I still have my times, Grace. There have been a few days that I just couldn't show up for work because my head was replaying ugly war scenes. There were nights I stayed awake as long as possible so I wouldn't fall asleep and have nightmares. Some days I get so depressed that I don't want to get out of bed.

"Like I said, I have been blessed to work for my dad. He won't fire me if I don't show up! Dad is a war vet himself, so he understands and has been patient with me. Of course, I still go to counseling when I feel the need.

"However, with all that goes through your head, I think the guilt is the worst." Jerry's eyes watered at that statement.

"Guilt? About what?" That didn't make any sense to Grace.

"There's lots of guilt, Grace. You see a friend blown to pieces, and not only does your heart break for him and his family, but you feel guilty because you didn't do anything to stop it — or because he was killed and you weren't!

"I know, I know. It doesn't make sense, but it is very real. We were all in the same boat, fighting for the lives of others as well as our own. So why did some die and not others? I still hurt sometimes when I think of wonderful soldiers who didn't make it. Why am I here enjoying the company of a beautiful lady when they will never see their own kids again?" Jerry stared at the floor for a couple of moments.

He went on, "I know Tag feels that, too. The last month over there was the hardest. We lost half our guys. You always wonder *'Why them and not me?'* I have to say, that's when most turn to alcohol, but I refused. I can tell you, it hasn't been easy, but I know alcohol isn't the answer and will cause me more problems than I already have.

"I'm not saying I'm a saint, by any means, Grace. I could bury my depression in a bottle without thinking about it some nights. But I also know if I did, it would be a long road to get back, and I am just too lazy to do that." Jerry always put a little humor into even the worst situation. They both chuckled.

"You just have to be patient. Tag will come around. I have seen guys who are in much worse shape than he is make a full circle to recovery. He'll make it, Grace. He'll make it because I know he loves you more than his own life."

"I know, I know. I know he will. I am just talking like a protective mother." Grace patted her stomach.

"Speaking of which, Grace, you *are* going to be the perfect mother. Never doubt that! Tag will come around. Just think: The moment he sees his son's tiny face will probably change everything!"

"I hope so, Jer. I hope so. Anyway, not that I don't love for you to stop by anytime, but why are you here?"

"I have the day off. Well, not exactly off, because I should be home studying, but I needed a little fresh air, and what better place to get it than with the most beautiful..."

"Yeah, yeah. So you didn't have to work or have a class today. Is what you're saying?" Grace enjoyed the compliments but never took them seriously.

"Right. No class today," Jerry said, but he had that 'I wanted the day off' smile on his face.

"Well, I love that you stopped by, but the morning is half over, and I have to call a cab and go to the main post office downtown. Tag forgot to mail our taxes last week after he picked them up from the accountant. Now, *today* is the deadline, and he told *me* to do it. I can't even drive our car any longer because I have to move the seat back so far that I can no longer reach the pedals!" The frustration came back into her voice, but the comment made her smile.

"Grace, you are not calling a cab. I'll take you. Really! No excuses!"

He had been around to help her out with Tag ever since they'd both returned from Iraq. Jerry was always the one who cared when even Grace herself wasn't sure if she did any more.

"Thanks, Jerry. You are always my guardian angel. The main post office is so far away, but I do appreciate it. What would I have done without you all these months?" Grace couldn't believe the sweet gesture.

"No problem. Would I let my little nephew ride in some strange cab?" He nodded toward her stomach.

Grace patted her stomach and laughed, "Heavens, no! We couldn't have *that!* You keep this up, and I will name him Little Jerry."

"Oh, please don't. You know I hate my name. It really isn't the name so much as the rotten uncle I was named after!" Jerry gave a sigh just thinking about it.

He had told her and Tag about the family scandal. His Uncle Jerry Barker was the life of the whole family. Everyone loved him. That was the reason his father had named his only child after his beloved older brother.

Then, when baby Jerry was three years old, Uncle Jerry had been given life in prison for child pornography, rape, and the murder of one of his victims. After that, no one ever mentioned his name again. He was killed in prison six years later.

Then Jerry perked up and said, "I know! Since he is going to be a miniature of his daddy, name him Taglet!"

"Taglet? *Really?* Who would do that to a child?"

On the way out the door, Grace punched him in the arm as they both laughed.

CHAPTER

THREE

It would take a while to get to the main post office in Dallas, but all she had was time, and the ride was pleasant. *That is what good company will do for you*, she thought. *And, quite frankly, it is nice to be away from Tag for a change.*

Riding in Jerry's new Ford F-250 Crew Cab pickup was super comfortable, even in her condition, but

Grace always enjoyed teasing him about his choice of wheels.

"I can sure see why you don't have a wife, Jer. No woman would want to go out to dinner in a truck!" Both of them laughed.

"*Au contraire, mon amie!* This baby is a chick *magnet!*" Jerry teased. "I have to fight them off because only four women will fit in here at a time! My little four-wheeler's name is 'Gladys.' And before you ask, it is because I am just '*gladys*' I can be to have her!"

Both laughed long and hard until tears fell. It took several minutes before Grace could get back in control. Her smile was large and genuine.

"Speaking of chicks, are you still seeing Stephanie? She is not only pretty but smart, too." Grace wanted to see Jerry find someone he could be happy with.

"Yes, so far, sweet Stephanie has continued to put up with me. I can't think of any reason why, but I am most grateful." Jerry smiled.

Grace could tell he was in love with the lady, and she was so happy for him. She really liked Stephanie, too. She genuinely seemed to care about Jerry and not his father's money.

"Well, when are you going to pop the big question? A girl like Steph won't wait around forever, you know! There must be a line of men a mile long waiting for you to get out of their way!"

"Soon, oh mother of my incredibly handsome and smart nephew. Soon!" Jerry's joking around was always contagious. "You and Tag up for a wedding?"

The mention of Tag brought the atmosphere back down. Grace didn't answer, and they were quiet for a while.

After several quiet moments, Jerry asked her, "Grace, is it alright with you if we stop and have a cup of coffee on the way? There is something I want to show you."

Grace wasn't under any time constraint so she agreed. Jerry pulled into a small restaurant that was nearly empty for it being late morning. He came around to help her out of the truck and then leaned in and pulled an envelope out of the glove box.

Settled in the restaurant, after making small talk and getting coffee, Jerry said he needed to share something with her.

"It isn't pleasant, Grace, and for that I apologize in advance. But maybe it will help you with some of what you are going through." Jerry opened the envelope, pulled out several pieces of paper, and handed them to her.

Grace glanced at them and then back at Jerry. "Am I supposed to know this person, Jerry? I don't understand."

"Yes and no. You won't know his name, but you will know what he is writing about." Jerry looked down into his coffee and just stayed there, so Grace started to read.

Dear Mom,

I hate to contact you this way, but I couldn't bear to see the pain in your eyes again after my last visit.

You asked me on the phone last month why I left the Army. I couldn't get into it then. Maybe it will be easier to explain on paper than trying to talk about it.

I was thrilled to go into the Army. But my first tour in Afghanistan was really a wake-up call, for sure. No one likes to see war in action. But we were there to protect democracy and the lives of innocent people, so I managed to hang in there. During that tour, I lost a friend who stepped on an IED booby trap just 10 feet in front of me. If he hadn't been there, it would have been my foot that set it off.

Why is that, Mom? Why did he die and I didn't? When I look in the mirror, I sometimes see his face. The picture he would show me of his pretty wife sticks in my mind, too. They had a baby that he had never seen…a baby. I have to tell you, Mom, I have cried over that a lot.

Well, when we came back to the States for a while, it wasn't much better. We had guys who were really hurting over all the things they'd seen and done, but they were treated more like whiners.

They were really razzed for complaining about the ringing in their ears or the nightmares they were having. I had my own problems — not as bad, mind you, but I sure wasn't going to let anyone know. I didn't want anyone to think I was a softy like they treated the others. I feel bad about that now. I sympathized but did nothing to help support them.

Then came the call to go back to the Hell Hole for one more tour. I figured I would know what to expect, so I felt I could handle it. No one, Mom, no one could have prepared me for what happened during that tour.

One of the main things that comes to mind is

my good friend, Lester. You might remember him from boot camp, the tall blonde kid with the scar over his eye. We were always together and swore to have each other's back.

Mom, it was a day like any other. Hot and quiet. Treacherously quiet.

We were advancing, with me and Lester in the front, when a young boy started to run to us out of an earthen dwelling. He could not have been more than five years old. He didn't say a word — he just ran toward us. His arms were out like he needed a hug.

Both Lester and I started to move at the same time, but Lester held me back. He got up from his shelter and ran for the little boy. Others in our group were yelling to shoot him, that he wasn't safe! Just shoot him! It was horrible! Why would you want to shoot a little boy?

Lester smiled and picked him up and hugged him tight so he would know someone cared for him. That is when the bomb went off, Mom. Lester and the little boy blew into pieces. Just like that…One minute there, next minute gone. Lester and a little boy.

Mom, what kind of evil would do that to a little child? That is when things started going downhill for me. I saw it happen over and over again in my dreams. My best friend sending out love, then vaporizing......a little boy having no idea that those he thought were his friends had sent him out to die.

Well, things didn't get any better after that. I would wake up at night screaming for Lester or kicking at something — I don't even know what. I was seeing the enemy everywhere. Life was a living nightmare.

But then came the day when the world stopped for me.

We were approaching a small village. We believed we had scared the enemy away from there. Women and children were coming out of their huts and smiling at us. Not a man to be seen. We were within twenty yards when it happened, Mom.

The prettiest little girl, about three years old, with long black hair and eyes, came running at me with her arms open. She was laughing.

My group behind me started yelling to shoot. SHOOT! I didn't know what to do. Was this beautiful little child going to kill me, like the boy did Lester? Had I learned *nothing* from my friend's death?

The group kept cocking their guns and yelling, "Shoot!" There was chaos all around me. I raised my rifle and pulled the trigger. Everything instantly went silent and into slow motion. She fell backwards, oh so slowly, and the silence seemed like forever.

Then a scream came from a woman who came running for her little girl, but I beat her there. The child did not have a bomb on her or any other weapon. She was just running to join the group of men who had saved their village. And she had a bullet right between her open eyes.

They had to pull me off of the little girl. I'll be honest with you, Mom, I didn't know who I was or why I was there. Time stopped. My life stopped. To tell you the truth, it never really came back.

I don't remember much after that until I was on a plane for the States. They said I was a wounded warrior and I would get help. That was fine with me, 'cause I knew I sure needed it.

When we arrived at Austin, Texas. I was a PTSD Clinical Outpatient. We were treated worse than criminals, Mom. I swear. We were given every dirty duty to do and ignored like we were invisible!

They didn't care about our injuries, mental or physical. They just wanted to punish us for not being unfeeling, killing robots. One man had lost an arm and a leg, was in a wheelchair, and had to mop floors. MOP FLOORS, MOM! With one arm, moving a chair and a mop. He cried all day long. He pushed the mop, then the chair, the mop, the chair...

I couldn't take it anymore. But I had another option. Take the misery or ask to leave. They are always glad to kick 'the losers' out the back door.

So, anyway, I left some six months ago, as you know, and have been pretty much living on the streets.   Yeah, I know, Mom. I could have come home, but you don't understand. Your son no longer exists. What has taken his place is a man who can't stand to look at himself, can't sleep because of the nightmares, paranoid that every sound is the enemy, and every moment of the day he looks at the face of that pretty little girl who wanted a friend and got shot between the eyes.

Well, Mom, this letter has gone on too long. I had to explain all of this to you to let you know your son really does NOT exist anymore. And his broken, half-crazy, delusional replacement won't live much longer, either.

I wanted to say my goodbyes while I am still somewhat rational. No, I won't go kill myself tonight. But I know I will soon. I just don't know when. I am writing this letter and putting it in an envelope addressed to you.

If you are reading this letter, Mom, then I am gone. Please be happy for me.

The pain and mental anguish I feel are just too much to live with. Forgive me, but I just can't take it anymore. May the Lord forgive me.

Love forever,

Steven

"Jerry! Is this real?" Grace had tears running down her face, trying to absorb the information she'd just read.

"Oh, I'm afraid so. I knew Steven up until about five years ago; then I lost track of him. I received this letter from his mother about a year ago, after she had been informed Steven had cut his own throat and bled to death. I haven't had the nerve to show Tag yet, because

I didn't know how he would take it. He knew Steven — not as well as I did, but he knew him." Now Jerry let a tear fall.

"Two months later, Steven's Mom, this sweet widow in her late 40s, took a bottle of sleeping pills and didn't wake up. She left a note saying there wasn't any reason left for her to get up in the morning." Jerry folded the pages back up in his wallet and used the napkin on the table to stop his tears. But the pain he felt was reflected on his face.

"I didn't know it was this bad..." Grace's voice was barely above a whisper. *What was Tag thinking? Was he going to.....?* No, she wouldn't think of that. *He wouldn't do such a thing!* She just couldn't bear it.

They downed what was left of their coffee. Jerry paid and left a tip. He led Grace out to his truck, as she was still wiping the tears from her eyes.

They left the restaurant and headed on to the post office in silence. They both were buried in their own painful thoughts. Before she knew it, they were at their turnoff.

CHAPTER

FOUR

Leaving the highway and turning onto the frontage road, they could see how full the post office parking lot was. It took a while, but they found a space, and Jerry accompanied her into the sprawling building, buzzing with activity.

The brick-façade front entrance hid about four city blocks of metal buildings attached behind it. This building was the main office for all of the mail in the Dallas area to be delivered, sorted, and sent on its way. Though the counters were closed by early evening, the back areas worked 24/7 to make sure the mail was delivered in a timely manner. Mail trucks pulled into the underground garage in back. Everything operated like clockwork.

Once Grace was inside the front door of the building, she instinctively put her hand on her stomach for protection since there were so many people everywhere.

"I had hoped to be able to get in and out of here, but I can see that won't be happening." Grace frowned at Jerry. This crowd wasn't doing much for her sadness.

A sign hanging from a wall told her if she needed to get the taxes postmarked today, she would have to get in a certain line, which happened to be the longest one. *Of course. What a surprise,* she thought. She couldn't put it into any of the boxes since they wouldn't be getting postmarked until tomorrow. The signs made that clear. Reluctantly, she claimed her spot in the long line.

Jerry, not allowing the morbid mood to linger any longer, smiled at her and pointed to the chairs at the far side of the room. After she smiled back and nodded, he moved over where seating was available to wait until Grace was finished. It was a little after twelve noon by then.

A half hour later, the line had barely moved. It was obvious that people had other things to do besides just get their taxes stamped. Some had boxes to mail or to be picked up. Her feet started to hurt, and Baby Reynolds wasn't happy, either. Every few moments, he began turning one way or the other, causing feet, hands, knees, and elbows to go into several of Grace's body parts.

By the third time his foot made a noticeable movement near her belly button, she started to believe she would never get out of this post office. Her child was trying to rearrange her insides, and she was not feeling well.

"Looks like your baby is also tired of waiting." The young man standing in front of her nodded toward her stomach. He appeared about twenty or so, and had a brown messenger bag across his chest with a scarf around his neck. He was well built and tall. Grace took him for a student.

"Yeah, Striker didn't get much of a breakfast this morning."

"Striker? That's a nice strong name! I have a granola bar in my bag." He quickly pulled out a bar and handed it to her.

"No, no...I couldn't possibly ..." Embarrassed, she stepped backwards.

"I won't hear of it. Your baby needs it way more than I do." He patted his stomach. Grace took it after the baby gave her another big kick.

"Thank you." She opened the package and took a bite. The granola bar was definitely as good as it looked.

"I'm Tommy Lee Walters, at your service, ma'am." He gave a half bow and grinned.

"Grace. Grace Reynolds. And 'Striker' is the best name I have found so far, but it could be thrown out tomorrow!" She smiled and held out her hand. He shook it.

"I hope they start moving soon, or I will be late for my first class," Tommy moaned and gave a half grin.

Nailed it. He's a student, Grace thought to herself as she finished the granola bar. She'd always been good at reading people.

Patting her stomach, she grinned, "Well, I hope they start moving soon, or *my* son will be late to class!" Both laughed at her joke.

"What are you going to school for?" Grace figured if she was going to be stuck in line, she may as well talk with this pleasant young man.

"Fashion design."

"Really? I got my BFA in fashion from the Art Institute of California," Grace said, a bit surprised by his answer.

"Seriously? I'm going to the University of North Texas for mine."

"That's wonderful. I'm always glad to see men who care about fashion. I work at *Fashion & Form* Magazine."

"You're *that* Grace Reynolds? I *love* your articles." The admiration in Tommy's eyes was apparent. "Your column picture does NOT do you justice!" After his statement, his cheeks turned red, and he fell quiet out of embarrassment for a moment.

Grace didn't usually let people know she worked at the popular magazine, but he seemed like a nice guy, also into fashion, so she figured she would share with him.

She blushed as he complimented her and continued to praise some of the work she had done. When he finished, she asked him about his classes and what he saw himself doing after he graduated. They exchanged ideas and thoughts on the industry. It helped them both pass the time.

As they continued to talk about fashion, they moved slowly toward the front of the line. It wasn't how Grace had planned to spend the afternoon, but there wasn't any choice. At least the Lord had put her with a nice man to talk to.

She glanced over at the side to find Jerry, and saw that her friend had lain his head back against the chair, crossed his arms, and was sound asleep. Grace smiled to herself.

Yay, Jerry! This entire wait will seem like only a couple of minutes to him. I sure wish I could join him. I never seem to get enough sleep these days. She patted her stomach and smiled.

CHAPTER

FIVE

Fred Mason came through the door from the back hallway, taking in everything the United States Post Office wanted an outsider to see. A pleasant-looking, older gentleman, he was immaculately dressed in slacks, shirt, and a lightweight sweater. His thinning white hair was neatly combed. Fred liked to be neat and tidy.

Most of the business offices were back down the hall, like Passports,

International, and of course, the men's room, where he had just come from. It wasn't too easy for him, requiring a cane to get around due to an arthritic leg, but he made it work okay.

Getting into the tax line, he found the amount of people interesting. No doubt about it: Tax day was the busiest day of the year for post offices around the country. Fred knew today would be busy, but as a widower, he would rather be here, with a bunch of people to talk to, than at home alone.

"This happens to be the first mail sorter used when this post office opened." The young woman stood in front of an old, brown sorting machine sitting out for people to see. She pointed out different aspects of the sorter to the gentleman beside her. It was encased in glass and sitting on a metal rolling cart.

"That actually isn't one of the originals. *They* were blue. They replaced them with the green ones after about five years. *That* one would have been put in approximately seven years after we opened." Fred was smiling and quietly talking to the man who was standing in front of him.

The man turned around and whispered back that it was a shame the new employees didn't know that kind of stuff. Fred just smiled and nodded.

Fred knew all about the post office he was standing in. He had worked in this building for more than forty years. When Fred turned 68, they'd made him retire. That was a year ago, and he still couldn't believe he didn't have to get up and come to work anymore.

There was a place in the front with a fax and copying machines. Vending machines offered a variety of items to help you with your mail.

The line moved slowly by framed stamps displayed on the wall. Fred looked at each one. He had spent so much time in this post office that he wouldn't think of going anywhere else to send off his mail. It was a little out of his way, but ever since his darling wife, Elizabeth, had died two years ago, he had plenty of time on his hands.

"They are interesting," a young man said as he came up to him by the display.

"Yes, they are." Fred turned toward him. "I used to work here. I saw many different stamps come and go through the years. I was always amazed at the wonderful creativity of them all."

The young man smiled before he moved away. Fred pushed up the sleeves of his sweater as he turned back to the stamps. *That young man will never know the memories of stamps that I have. What a shame.*

~ ~ ~

Jawad Bazzi definitely didn't want to be at the post office on the busiest day of the year. Trouble was all it would mean for him. Ever since 9/11, Americans didn't really like to see Muslims in public places. Jawad was well aware of it, but he didn't have a choice.

Yes, he had mailed in his taxes a month ago. However he'd received a letter that there were issues with his passport, directing him to come in for a meeting today. How he wished it were on any other day than this one. *This country takes the money I worked hard for, and now they are trying to jerk me around because I want to leave.*

What could be wrong with my passport? Just because I want to go back to Iraq to see my family doesn't mean I am a terrorist.

They keep insulting me and my family by throwing it in my face that one of my brothers had been known to make bombs for various groups.

So what? What does that have to do with me? I am sick of being treated like I am sub-human by these spoiled Americans.

He messed with the tie around his neck for the hundredth time and straightened his suit jacket on his five-foot-eight slender frame. Jawad didn't like dressing like an American, but there was little choice. At least for now. That would change when he got home.

He searched the directory hanging on the wall. The paper stated he needed to meet with a 'Mrs. Stratton,' yet the board showed no such person on it. He decided to head through the door and down the hall to the passport office, but he didn't have time to look before a security guard came up to him, taking his arm a little too firmly.

"Can I help you, *sir?*" The guard's voice dripped with sarcasm.

Jawad looked at the man standing to the side of him and could tell this wasn't someone concerned about one of the visitors being lost. He was concerned that Jawad was up to no good.

"I'm fine." Jawad used his left hand to remove the guard's hand from his arm. Hate showed on his face. "Don't touch me again."

"Oh, did I invade your personal space, *sir*?"

"As a matter of fact...."

"I never *meant* to do any harm."

"It's obvious what you *meant*, but I think it is best if you go find another person to bother." Jawad's hatred for this man was also obvious.

"Bother? I'm *bothering* you?" This time the guard's loud voice got the attention of the people standing around.

CHAPTER

SIX

Emil Brown owned the gym a couple of blocks away. He'd started out as a personal trainer until he could afford his own place. People didn't tend to give him too hard of a time, since his muscles were evident, even through his long sleeve shirt. He had stopped to drop off a package on his way into work and was shocked at the crowd inside.

"Yes, you *are* bothering me. All I want is to find the passport office. I have a meeting. Keep your hands off me, or you will regret it!"

Emil could see the Middle-Eastern man was trying to get away from a guard.

One thing that Emil disliked more than not being able to work out in the morning was people who were racist. Being African-American, he had dealt with his share of these idiots his whole life. Now, whenever he saw it happening, he tried to intervene.

"Excuse me," Emil said as he stepped up to the foreigner. "The passport office is through that door, down the hall about half-way. There is a big sign hanging from the ceiling with an arrow."

The foreigner nodded his head slightly at Emil. "Thank you." He gave a look of pure hatred to the security guard, taking a step away from him.

"It's nice to see some people in this country aren't stupid."

Emil gave him a small nod back as he walked away.

"Can you believe they allow them people into this country?" The security guard called after Emil and continued, "After everything they did? After 9/11?"

Emil didn't have time to deal with the guard. He knew a lot of Americans felt that way, and had to admit sometimes he did too. Emil headed toward one of the short lines at the counter with his package. With only five people ahead of him, he would be back to work in less than a half hour.

This was the closest post office for a couple of miles. Otherwise, he wouldn't even had thought of coming into this place.

Recent memories brought anger back to his heart. That low-life Frank Benson worked here, somewhere back in the mail room. He always bragged about how he had all these bennies from the government, when he was really just getting Emil's tax dollars. But when that white-ass stole his wife, Sarah, hatred replaced anger.

Emil wanted revenge and he would get it. Sooner than later. How could she leave him for a white man? Let alone one who worked in a post office?

That jerk wasn't going to get away with what he'd done. Not by a long shot. Emil was going to make him pay. He had friends who were always willing to help him out, especially when it came to white men. Sarah would see the error of her ways, but it would be too late.

~~~

Grace and Tommy had become quite friendly as they were making their way through the line. After they talked about their common interest in fashion, it wasn't long before the conversation turned to their personal lives. That was when Tommy revealed to Grace that he was gay.

She wouldn't have guessed it by the way he acted, dressed, or even talked. Almost six foot, well filled out, he looked more like a construction worker. Not that a construction worker couldn't be gay, but still...

Unfortunately for Tommy, he said his family wasn't supportive of his lifestyle and it had caused a huge rift in their relationship. They had kicked him out and had not spoken to him since.

"I understand completely," Grace rubbed her stomach, feeling more pressure than normal but brushed it off as due to being on her feet all morning.

"My parents weren't exactly thrilled when I chose to marry a Marine. I was raised by high-society parents. It didn't matter that I was in love — they were afraid of what their friends would think of them, having a lowly Marine son-in-law. They felt my husband was below my social level. It became so bad, I told them to take what their friends thought over what I wanted, and I walked out. I haven't spoken to them since, and that has been for more than five years now."

"Your husband's a Marine? Was he over *there*?" Tommy's look of concern was genuine.

"He did two tours of duty and was on the bomb patrol. He saw a lot, which, of course, explains...." Grace realized she was just about to tell a stranger about how messed up her marriage was. Without any warning, the room suddenly started to spin.

"Grace, are you okay?" Tommy reached for her hand, which was a blessing, since she felt like she was going to fall over.

"Dizzy."

Tommy looked at the person behind him, who nodded his head to let him know he would hold their place in line. He helped her over to a small group of chairs, located along the one wall.

"I'll stay in line; when you see me get to the front, come up." Tommy made sure she was comfortable and went back to the line.

He would check on her now and then but allowed her to sit and relax while the line made its slow progress. The couple of times she looked at Jerry, a few chairs away, he was still sleeping.

She would get a chuckle out of this. Oh, the stories she would be able to tell on him!

When Tommy reached the counter, he waved Grace over and allowed her to be in front.

"How can I help you?"

Grace felt sorry for the girl behind the counter, whose name tag said, "Hi, I'm Melinda." She was very pretty but looked exhausted and still had the majority of the day to work since it was only about one-thirty by then. She handed the girl her envelope, with a smile on her face, hoping the friendly look would help her out.

"Your husband is in the military? I see your return address has his rank on it."

Grace answered, "No. He has been out for more than ten months now. We just haven't ordered any new ones."

"Okay, I will stamp it and get it moving for you. Do you have anything else, a package or a pickup?

After Grace shook her head, she stated, "I have been standing here for three hours, and I have to take a break. I will try to find someone else to take over. Otherwise, those people behind you will have to wait..."

Grace looked at the girl in pity. After standing in line all this time, the people behind her would not be happy. But what could the poor girl do? She looked exhausted, and Grace felt sorry for her.

She smiled and stepped out of line just as the "on a break" sign went up. The people behind her groaned, and some started yelling.

Before waking Jerry, she called Tag at home, hoping he might be sober, but the phone just rang and rang. When Grace hung up, someone yelled at her for getting served before the clerk took a break. She turned around but didn't have time to deal with someone being rude.

Grace looked at the bleached blonde who seemed so angry that she looked dangerous!

CHAPTER

SEVEN

Marta Salinas was one of those Hispanic women who didn't have a beautiful face, but there was no doubt about her perfect body. She worked as a stripper and was the one who got most of the tips by the end of the night. Marta had learned the right moves to entice men early in life.

With enough makeup on, men didn't really notice her plainness. When she arrived at the post office and discovered the long line, Marta walked up to the middle of the line, and a bald-headed man allowed her to jump in front of him, while he looked her up and down. She didn't care. That's what men do.

What's with the line? She only had to drop off Sam's tax returns. They were not married, but he used her and her son as dependents. Marta's son, 15-year-old Larry Miguel, was with her.

It wasn't her choice to drag along the teen. Her boyfriend, Sam, made her bring him. He said she needed to spend some time with him. *Really? He never cared before.* In fact, he and Larry hated each other. *And how does standing in line constitute spending time together?*

Marta and Sam hadn't been getting along lately. He'd told her she wouldn't be worth a dime to him in a year or two. At thirty, Marta knew she was pushing a time when stripping wouldn't work anymore, but would he really get rid of her for that? Sam was supposed to love her.

Her son was black, like Sam, but they weren't related. Larry was the result of Marta being raped by some gang member when she was fourteen.

Marta looked at her son, who was already taller than she was. *Oh, well — that's ancient history. I have made a good living with this body of mine. Not that I have a dime to my name. Sam sees to that.*

She was due to strip at a private party in less than thirty minutes, and some pregnant woman was holding up the line. And what was she going to do with her boy while she was stripping? Marta was getting more irritated by the moment.

She pushed a button on her cell phone to call the man who'd set up the party.

"I'm sorry, Harvey. The line here is ridiculous." She flipped her long, bleached hair as if to make a statement. The people around her moved away a little. "I'll be there as soon as I can."

Emil was one of the few people who didn't move away. When she looked toward the side, their eyes met, and she gave him a smile. He didn't smile back, but he didn't look away, either. Emil looked at her African-American son and then back at her. Marta felt that was a good sign. *See, he's black, like you. That must mean I like black men.*

She liked what she saw when she looked at Emil, but right now she just needed to get out of this line and get to work. Private parties generated bigger tips, and she didn't want to miss out on a dime. She thought, *The fact that my son is black may give me an 'in' to chat with him later.*

"You get taken care of because you are preggy?" Marta yelled up to the front. Larry laughed. "Then she takes a break? What's with that?"

The pregnant woman turned around and looked at her. Not that it did any good. The window sign said it would be closed for 10 minutes.

"Can you believe her?" Marta said to no one in particular. "Just because she's pregnant, she gets taken care of. Now we have to wait longer in line."

This time, the pregnant lady at the front didn't even turn around.

~ ~ ~

Not caring what the rude lady behind her in line was saying, Grace turned to leave, but one step was as far as she got.

(((((BOOM!))) (((BOOM! BOOM!)))))

The room erupted! The explosion of sound was deafening, and time stood still. Silence filled her head as everything moved in slow motion. The blasts twisted Grace around from the counter and blew her down sideways, against the counter.

Slowly, ever so slowly, she began to fall. It seemed to take minutes for it all to happen, but she knew it was only seconds. When she finally hit the floor, she bounced a little, trying desperately to protect her stomach. She could hear nothing but the ringing in her ears.

Lying on the floor on her side, with her back to the counter, she could see people everywhere. The most incredible sight was the blood slowly flying all over the room. The majority of the people were lying on the floor. She had been hit with some little things flying through the air, so she closed her eyes and curled up in a ball to make as small a target as possible.

Grace was afraid to move for a long time. When she finally opened her eyes, Tommy was on his hands and knees, covering her body from the falling debris. Frightened and thankful, she reached up and grabbed him in a bear hug. That's when her ears popped and her hearing returned. The reality around her finally soaked in.

"Don't worry, Grace. I've got you." Tommy appeared frightened as well but wouldn't move from on top of her. When all finally became silent, he helped her off the floor.

"Tommy, what happened?" Grace whispered. She was completely stunned and in fear for her baby.

"Well, either an airplane slammed into the building, or someone set off a few bombs!" Tommy said. "Remember, it wasn't that long ago that someone set a bomb off at the Dallas Police Department. What — a couple of years, maybe?"

Grace *did* remember the Police Department bombing. *Could it be? Did someone really bomb the post office?* The entire front of the building had collapsed, eliminating a way to exit in that direction. Windows disappeared, and the darkness was frightening. She could barely see the blood trickling from Tommy's head, where he had been hit.

"You're bleeding!" Grace reached for the wound, but Tommy moved her hand.

"It's okay," Tommy wiped at the blood dripping down his forehead. "The important question is: Are *you* and the baby okay?"

"No, I...uh, well, I have a few cuts on my arms and legs. The blood is nothing, really. The wounds are minor." Grace was as relieved as Tommy.

Emergency lights came on and flickered, and an ear-piercing alarm was going off somewhere to her right, while all around her she could hear people moaning and crying but still couldn't see them through the smoke and debris. It reminded her of those 'end of the world' movies that played on the science fiction channels. Finally, the alarm ended, leaving the scene in silence. Minimal lighting still flickered, making it hard to see, but at least there was *some* light.

Tommy went with Grace as she looked for her friend, Jerry. It took some time to step over the debris in order to get a mere fifteen feet away. The chairs were no longer in the same place, and the bloody bodies of victims were everywhere. They continued to move a piece of the ceiling or furniture, until they found him.

"JERRY! Oh, no — oh nooooo!" Grace moved as close to her friend as she could get. "Jerry, Jerry! Don't die on me! NO!"

He was unconscious and bleeding profusely. There was little sign of life. It was obvious to them both that Jerry was near death.

Grace broke down and cried while Tommy held her. They used Tommy's scarf to wrap around the huge gash in one of Jerry's legs, and Grace tore up the skirt of her dress for strips to bind Jerry's head and arm wounds.

He was barely breathing, but he *was* breathing. It didn't look like he would make it. She knew it but refused to accept it.

CHAPTER

EIGHT

Tag Reynolds woke from a dream in which a phone kept ringing and ringing. He looked around and realized he was on the living-room couch but couldn't remember how he got there. He staggered across the living room and into the kitchen.

His head was still fuzzy from the night before. He knew exactly what would help. He opened the fridge but was shocked to discover the two bottles of alcohol that he remembered being there last night were gone.

Why couldn't Grace have gotten him more? Knowing her, she probably dumped them down the sink. Nothing like having a wife who doesn't care about her husband. All she cares about is that kid she's carrying.

Having a kid seemed like a good idea at the time, but with his nightmares and flashbacks, he didn't have time to deal with Grace and her moods. *Why can't she see that?*

Even worse, when the baby is born, all it will do is cry all the time. I may have to find somewhere else to live by then. This just isn't going to work out. Frustrated, Tag headed upstairs to the bedroom.

His anger faded away when he stopped at the top landing. The medals, awards, and pictures of him in uniform were all on display on the wall in the upstairs hallway. Grace was always so proud of his accomplishments. *If she only knew the things I saw and had to do while over in that hell hole. But then again, I would never want her to see those things.*

Tears started to form in his eyes as he recalled the reason for each of the medals. Tag slowly ran his fingers over each photo, hurting at the friends standing beside him who didn't come home.

He went into the bedroom and sat on the edge of the bed and cried. The pain came from deep within his gut.

Tag knew he was a big disappointment to Grace. How could he not be? Drunk all the time; can't even get a job to support his family. Add to that, a baby was coming soon.

What would his son think of his drunken old man? His life was in shambles, and he didn't know how it had happened. But the *how* didn't really matter, did it? It just *was*. He was a worthless, no good, drunk.

He reached down underneath the box springs and pulled out a black case. Once opened, he removed his 9mm pistol. Tag stared at it for a long while, turning it in different directions. The light from the window would reflect off the gun at a certain angle and would cause a flash of war memories to come flooding back. He was in agony and knew he couldn't take much more. The memories, the drinking, not able to work, the disappointment in Grace's eyes...he couldn't take it...he didn't want to live this way anymore.

He pointed the pistol to his head.

This is what I need to do, thought Tag. *Grace will be able to get on with her life and find a good man to raise my child right.*

It would've been easy to pull the trigger, and Tag knew it. He ordered himself to do it, moving his finger tighter on the trigger. Then, in the corner of the dresser mirror, he saw a picture of his wedding to Grace.

Beautiful, elegant, Grace. The gorgeous high-society girl who walked away from her rich lifestyle to make a life with him. Because she loved a mere Marine, her parents disowned her. But Grace didn't care. She gave up everything to marry Tag Reynolds, the love of her life.

He stared at the picture for a long time. How long was impossible to say. Forever or a few moments, it didn't matter.

Startled back to reality by a loud "thunk" on the floor, Tag realized he had let go of his gun. It had fallen from his hand and hit the floor.

With his face in his hands, he cried again until his whole body hurt. Devastation was all he felt. He lay back on the bed to think, but quickly dozed off into a dreamless sleep.

An hour later, Tag awoke. Getting up, he spotted the gun on the floor. Suddenly, he was horrified at what could have happened. He really *had* wanted to kill himself! He had to do something about his life. He *had* to — but what?

He cleaned the bathroom, then Tag forced himself to shower and get dressed in clean clothes. He stared into the mirror after shaving and combing his hair. When was the last time he'd cleaned himself up? He couldn't remember. Something had to give. If he wasn't going to kill himself, then he would have to straighten up somehow, because he wasn't going to continue to live like this!

Returning downstairs, he sat in front of the television. Since he'd come back from overseas, he hadn't been able to find a single job, and they were running through their savings way faster than expected. If it hadn't been for Grace's job, they wouldn't have made it this far. It wouldn't be too much longer before they had nothing.

Having a drink entered his mind. He turned on the television in the hopes that it would distract him from the alcohol, at least until he could get Grace to go get him some. One drink wouldn't hurt. Right?

Flipping through the channels, he hoped he could find some comedy, but the local news caught his attention. It was an aerial shot of Dallas, and large amounts of smoke could be seen rising above the buildings.

"Not more than an hour ago, this station received a report of a suspected terrorist attack. It would seem there has been several explosions at the location of Dallas's main post office, just off the highway.

"Police are still arriving, while fire trucks and ambulances are on their way. As you can see behind me, the entire front entrance has collapsed and disappeared. There are some people lying on the ground around the front who apparently were just getting ready to enter the building, but it is impossible to tell if they are alive.

"Police have cordoned off the area and won't let anyone get close. We will keep you informed as we find out any further information. This is Marion Anderson. Back to the station."

"NO! No, No, NO!" Tag jumped up from the couch as he continued to stare at the TV.

"NO! GRACIE!" Running his hands through his hair, he wandered around the room, keeping his eyes on the TV in case they came back with more information.

"I have to get to her! She needs me!" Thinking out loud, he grabbed his billfold and keys. *Please don't let her be hurt, God. Please!*

Sitting behind the wheel of their car, Tag couldn't think straight. His mind was playing war games with him. It didn't take long for him to realize he was in no condition to drive.

CHAPTER

NINE

In a panic, Tag was able to get a taxi. The news about the explosions at the post office was on every radio station as he tried to get to his wife. She had tried to call him at some point in the morning, and he cursed his decision to drink so much the night before. And the night before that. And the night before that.

Maybe if he wasn't drinking all the time, he would have remembered to take the taxes to the post office himself, and Grace and their baby wouldn't be in danger. *Oh, God! Please let her be okay!*

Tag pressed Grace's name again on his phone's speed dial in an attempt to make some connection with her. He needed to know she was okay.

Things had been horrible between them the past few weeks, months really, with him deciding to deal with his depression by drinking instead of something productive. He couldn't possibly imagine this being the way things would end with him and his precious Gracie.

"The number you dialed is unavailable. Try your call again later." "Damn it." Tag slammed his fist into the back of the seat in front of him.

"Hey." The cabby looked at Tag in the rearview mirror. "No cursing in my cab. The Lord, Himself, is listening. If that's the way you want to be, I'll let you off here."

"Sorry, it won't happen again," Tag said, immediately ashamed. "Can we go any faster? My pregnant wife was supposed to be at the post office that has been bombed."

Through the rearview mirror, the man gave him a sad nod of understanding and pushed the pedal down a little further. As the cab drew closer, they got stuck in the traffic jam of people trying to get to or away from the same place. They were still about a mile from the post office.

"Thanks, but I'll get out here and walk the rest of the way," Tag said as he handed the driver money.

"May God be with you, mister," the driver said and waved away the money.

Tag nodded his head, thankful that there were still some kind and caring people left in this world. It was the only money he had on him.

He jogged four blocks and could see the smoke coming from where the post office was located. Estimating another three blocks, he saw the panic in the people's faces as he got closer.

A young woman was trying to get a child into a car, but the child wasn't cooperating. Tag stopped and was about to offer help when a big, burly man came barreling down steps and to the woman.

Getting out of the area is a great idea, Tag thought. *At least until we know more about what happened and who is involved. This could just be the tip of the proverbial iceberg. God, did I come home to die in another war here?*

Only one more block to go, Tag thought to himself. Then everything went silent for one second before another explosion shattered through the air, quickly followed by a second. The ground trembled, and a few seconds later, the heat came whooshing at Tag.

More bombs! He went flat on the ground like he was taught. Grabbing for his gun, Tag suddenly realized he was not in combat. Slowly looking around to be sure, he got to his feet and started to run toward the smoke, which had doubled since he'd last looked up.

He pressed Grace's name again on his phone. Busy. Off, and try again. Busy. Off, and try again. Busy. He kept repeating this action as he made his way closer and closer to the destruction he was afraid to see. People were yelling and running toward him, trying to get out of the area, while he desperately needed to get in.

~~~

Grace opened her eyes to find herself on the floor of the post office again. There was fire everywhere, with smoke and dust so thick it was keeping her from seeing anything past her own body. She started choking and realized she was cradling Jerry in her arms. She knew he was dead at this point, but she wasn't about to let go.

"Grace? Grace? Where are you?"

She recognized the voice but wasn't sure where it was coming from. Then she saw Tommy's face appear from the cloud of smoke.

"Grace! Are you okay?"

"I don't know." She moved around to see if there were any signs of additional injuries. Her shoulders were stiff, and small pieces of debris had left more flesh wounds, but other than that, it seemed she was okay. She placed her hand on her protruding stomach and was grateful for Baby Reynolds' kicking his displeasure of the situation.

"At least I know why I call him 'Striker.'" Grace gave a half smile.

She noticed Tommy looking up, and she followed suit. The ceiling didn't look sturdy where they were standing. It was bowing, with small pieces flipping off.

"I think we should move," he said. "The last bombs seemed to come from the back end of the building. Whoever is responsible for these bombs knew what they were doing. The first ones shut off any escape from the front. And I'll bet the second round brought down the back end, closing off the exit from that direction. It's not looking good, but for now, we need to get somewhere safer."

"I agree with you, Tommy, but I won't leave Jerry. Even if he is dead, he has to come with us, or I won't go."

Tommy hesitated a moment, and Grace watched as he looked first at the man in her arms and then back at her.

He then nodded and helped her up again. He told her he would go looking for something they could carry Jerry on.

Grace heard a crash not far from where she stood. After a couple of minutes, Tommy came back with the metal cart that had held the old sorting machine, which was now in shambles.

"All the glass is gone," Tommy said to her. "The sorting machine was too heavy. I couldn't pick it up so I had to slide it off onto the floor and out of the way. This board that held it is strong. Plus, being three feet tall, this case is on wheels."

Grace thanked him and was thankful with the effort he'd put into helping her. This cart was going to be as good as it gets for right now.

The smoke was getting thinner. She hoped this meant that the fire that caused it was either out or about to be. Tommy rolled the cart up to Jerry, lifted him up, and laid the man on it. He wrapped him into a fetal position so he would fit.

"I don't think he is alive, either," Tommy said, "but I am sure not going to argue about it. Let's go."

Pulling the cart with one hand, he took her hand with the other, leading her back across the lobby space until he felt they were in as safe a spot as he could find. Getting the cart around the large rubble and over smaller pieces took some time, but Tommy made it work.

Passing by the counter where she was talking with the pretty girl, Melinda, just minutes earlier, Grace saw her lying flat on her back, eyes open, with a large piece of glass stuck deep into her forehead. There was no doubt she was dead. Grace knew instantly if the first blast had not knocked her down so suddenly, that piece of glass would be in the back of *her* head instead. Melinda never got the chance to walk away for her break.

Why did God take such a young thing? It should have been me! She never had a chance. God, why her? Grace was about to fall apart.

Oh, Lord! I'm feeling guilt. Just like Jerry said! I feel guilty because someone else died when it should have been me. Oh, Tag — please forgive me! I understand now. God, help me and help me to help him. Grace's thoughts added to her already falling tears.

It didn't take long to see that Tommy was right about the effects of the explosions. The first three bombs took out the front part of the building, with the ceilings and walls coming down and closing off any escape. The second two seemed to come from another part of the building but were just as terrifying. Bodies were everywhere. Some who had survived the first bombs didn't make it through the last two.

God, what am I to do? Her world had turned upside down in a split second. What was important a few moments ago, no longer mattered.

A few people were crying or bleeding or both. Others were lying either unconscious or dead. She wanted to help each and every one of them but knew there was no way of doing so. She couldn't even help herself. What would she have done without Tommy?

Once they made it to the opposite wall, Tommy helped her sit down on a small bench. He took the spot next to her, watching the chaos around them, the entire scene looking like a bad zombie movie. With Jerry parked in front of her, she kept wiping at his face and arms, trying to mop up blood, but it didn't seem to help much.

"Tommy, what can we do? There have been five explosions. What if there are more? Are we going to die in here?"

CHAPTER

TEN

Sirens continued. Mass confusion was the most common facial expression of those gathering outside to watch the horror. The front of the post office had come down, leaving no entrance or exit available. Some of the onlookers seemed overwhelmed at the thought of the people dead or trapped inside.

The police were quick to respond. They arrived only moments after the first bombs had gone off. The police officers had visions of September 11th as they barricaded the roads.

The television crews weren't too far behind the police and stood as tight to the barricade as they could in order to get the best video of the scene. One of the television reporters, Marion Anderson, watched everything to be ready to report what she saw.

Fire trucks arrived and were parked in place. Water started flying over parts of the building. Anderson watched the chaos while the firefighters tried to get their trucks through all the people who had decided this was a spectator sport instead of the site of a tragedy. Firefighters jumped out of the trucks and were pouring water on the fire in just minutes.

Ambulances arrived and were lined up, waiting for someone to get out alive.

While waiting, they were treating spectators going into shock.

No survivors from the front of the building had been discovered yet. However, four bodies had been removed, and the news media made sure to let the audience know. Some postal workers had been running around from the back of the building to see what had happened.

No one had tried to enter the main post office from the back side due to the fear and confusion. After the second bombs went off, they discovered it was no longer an option.

Ms. Anderson watched all that was going on around her and didn't miss an opportunity to inform the public. It was such a terrible tragedy, and someone had to let the public know what was going on.

She also had to make sure she didn't break down or shed a tear while on camera. That was the sign of an amateur, and she couldn't afford to make that mistake. Not now. Not ever.

"Hello. This is Marion Anderson. As we have reported, some of those killed appeared to be entering the front of the building when the first bombs went off. Firefighters and police are trying to get to each one. At last count, four had been found, all dead. Their remains have been removed to the county coroner's office, we are told. At this time there are no identifications for those killed in the blasts.

"Police have just informed us they received some sort of a warning a few days ago that stated for them to 'Be prepared for chaos times ten!' No further information was given so the police did not have anything to go on. If the person was talking about this event, the police say they can expect five more bombs to go off, since five have already wreaked their havoc.

"That's it for now. We will be back as further news develops. This is Marion Anderson. Back to the newsroom."

~~~

The second set of bombs caused flying debris to be thrown into the watching crowd, causing some minor injuries. Tag watched as people were screaming and running in all directions, sending the already crazy scene into something he didn't think the police would be able to get back under control. More than fifty officers were present, but Tag wasn't sure that would be enough.

He was running toward the post office as fast as he could. This was the first time since he'd come home that Tag was thankful for his years in the service. Those years had given him the strength and stamina to run — at least what the booze hadn't taken from him.

People, trying desperately to get away from the building that had become ground zero, were running toward him and had no reservations about pushing someone in front of them out of the way. Tag literally had to battle his way through the panicked crowd.

When Tag reached the corner, flat panel televisions in a TV repair shop window grabbed his attention. All the sets were playing one of the local stations and reporting on the post office explosions. He began to shake, and sweat poured down his back. Staring at the TV, he was transported back to the war. Bombs, screaming, dying. *Run, Tag, run! Where? Where can I hide?*

Tag swung around to see others watching the TVs in the window. He plowed through them to get away and ran across the street, where he hit the pavement. He felt his life threatened! He shook and held his hands over his ears while he talked out loud to himself that he wasn't overseas. He was home...home...home... It was a few minutes before he could focus on the people around him and not the enemy he thought they were.

"I can't do this. I can't save her. I can't even save myself!" The fight was going on in Tag's head. He felt weak, useless. Again, he wanted to die. Then his mind went to that beautiful wedding picture he had looked at just this morning. Gracie. Gorgeous Gracie.

Get it together, Tag. You have to save her. You have to! As weak as he felt, he got back up off the ground, crossed the street, and returned to watching the TVs spit out the latest horrific disaster. Though his heart was pounding, he was able to keep it together. News was back on the television, and he gave it his full attention.

"This is Marion Anderson. For those of you just tuning in, earlier today the main Dallas post office became a scene of horror as three bombs went off apparently just inside the main entrance. Since then, a second attack, with two bombs exploding near the rear of the building, has occurred, and we were here to record it for you.

"We are going to play the video now. Please be advised, it is not recommended for children."

The pretty blonde reporter turned to look at the monitor as the video played.

"The local authorities don't know who is responsible, and no one has come forward so far... They are asking for anyone with information to please call the number on your screen. They would also like me to let you know the area is being heavily restricted, so please stay where you are, and avoid this area.

"This is Marion Anderson. Back to the newsroom."

Tag didn't care if they were restricting the area or not. He was going to be there until his wife and child came out. And they would come out alive. They just *had* to. He felt his own life depended upon their survival, as well.

CHAPTER

ELEVEN

Grace and Tommy were still huddled under the area that appeared to be the safest, but the last blasts had done severe damage. The ceiling had started to rain down more pieces of plaster, and Grace could now see cracks going across the whole area. It was becoming harder and harder to keep Jerry from getting hit with debris.

"We are okay. We are okay. We are okay." It was Tommy whispering, mostly to himself.

Grace tried to hug Tommy a little closer, but he started to rock as he repeated those three words to himself. She was scared also, but she needed to keep her cool if she was going to get out of this mess.

She looked around and watched the few people still able to pick themselves up after these second explosions. Grace wasn't even sure where it had originated but knew that she and Tommy had been talking about what to do next when suddenly everything shook and things started to fly.

She noticed an African-American male walk over to that blonde Hispanic woman, the one that was so rude in line, and help her to her feet. The child was also African-American, so Grace wondered if the man was her husband. He placed his hand on her elbow, gently talking the whole time. They headed toward Grace and Tommy, helping a couple people off the floor along the way.

"My name is Emil. Is everyone okay?" The black man was the first to speak.

He looked back over his shoulder at the dead and dying. As it stood, Grace could see only five or six people alive.

"I'm Tommy, and the pregnant lady here is Grace." Tommy made sure everyone knew about her condition, as if they couldn't tell for themselves. "And Jerry here is unconscious. We are moving him around on this cart."

All eyes turned toward Jerry. Someone said, "He looks dead to me."

Grace said, "He is unconscious and has a damaged leg, but if we can get him some help..." Grace knew she was lying, but she wasn't going to let anyone remove her friend.

"The only thing all of us need is to get out of here." She actually said it with a smile, but the Hispanic woman just glared at her. *Guess she remembers I got served and she didn't. Not that it makes any difference now.*

"Emil, why don't you see if you can get us out of here? You could maybe lift some of those big pieces." Tommy pointed toward the pieces of ceiling that had completely covered the only doorway to the outside.

"Those aren't moveable — you know that. I think it's best if we just sit tight and wait for them to rescue us. It shouldn't be too long," Emil said.

"They won't be coming in any time soon." Grace turned to Tommy. "My husband said that they never go into a building that had a bomb go off until they were sure it is safe. We've already had five bombs go off, and there could be more."

"Hush. Things will be okay. You need to stay calm," Emil stated but realized too late it was a stupid thing to say.

Grace said as quietly and calmly as she could, "Help is *not* coming any time soon. Get that through your heads. We will have to find a way out by ourselves, or we just wait until another bomb goes off and we are all dead."

~ ~ ~

Stunned, Fred made his way through the debris, which was scattered everywhere. He used his free hand to wipe off what he could from his clothes, but they weren't close to being clean any more. His other hand was grasping the cane he needed for walking. He bumped into a man who had been bent over.

"Are you okay?" Fred asked the man as he righted himself. This gave him a good look at the stranger, and he took a step back. It was one of those Middle-Eastern foreigners. He had to admit, he was more than a little taken aback.

"Yeah," Jawad replied to the older gentleman. "We seem to be the only ones still alive here."

Jawad took a look around the area. He made his way to a pile of rubble that was covering a doorway leading to another area of the post office.

"I hear people talking! Help me with these pieces." He pointed to the rubble.

This foreigner is ordering me around? Fred was afraid to tell him "No." *What is that look on the man's face? Hatred? Maybe it's just determination. That has to be it, but...*

Fred wasn't the strong man he used to be, but he had no choice. Together the men worked on pulling piece after piece from the pile, until they had an opening. The sound of voices got louder.

"Why don't you see if you can get some water from that commissary on the other side? I'm sure these people would like to have something to drink."

Fred was okay with that. Besides, getting away from this guy was a great idea. He knew this building better than anyone. He still couldn't figure out how he had lived through that second set of blasts, let alone the first. Fred had a wound on his head. It was bleeding pretty well, though he didn't think it life threatening.

~~~

Once the old man had left, Jawad stuck his head in and found a group of about five or six people all gathered together. They were talking calmly, and some even seemed to be laughing a little.

Laughing? Stupid people. Americans are worthless. He gave one last look toward where the old man had headed and then crawled through the opening. He certainly didn't want anyone sneaking up behind him. He would help the people from that side get over on his side. That way, they would be where he could keep an eye on them.

~ ~ ~

Many employees closest to the back side of the post office had been injured by the second set of bombs while they were trying to figure out what had happened. Firefighters, and even the police, were helping the wounded who were able to get out from the back side of the building before it all collapsed.

Bandages and blood seemed to be everywhere as Tag finally reached the partitions that the police had put up. He looked around at all the wounded and knew this wasn't even a small piece of the devastation.

How did the people who were inside make it out? Was there anyone even still alive? Was the enemy still..... Focus!

Tag. Focus! You can't help Grace unless you focus! You need to stop!

"You need to stop." A policeman held his hand up to Tag, basically repeating what was already going through his mind. The difference was that Tag meant his *thoughts,* and this man meant his *body.*

"I'm a Marine. My pregnant wife is inside that building."

The police officer gave him a look of sorrow and waved him through. Tag wondered what the look was about. His wife and baby were going to be fine. Surely, a government building that big had sturdy construction.

The chances that his wife would be hurt were low. At least that was what he kept telling himself as he made his way through the people. It was better to think positive thoughts. Any other way, and he wouldn't be able to take another step.

A loud crash was heard. Everyone stopped, trying to figure out where it had come from. Tag saw a man running from the back end. When he got close enough to Tag, he was gasping for air and crying.

"They're dead. They almost made it. They're dead!"

Paramedics were trying to help him, as Tag watched.

"A few people were getting out a small hole left in the back side, when the whole wall collapsed, crushing them! Oh, my God in heaven! They were crushed to death...."

The paramedics led him away to an ambulance as he kept muttering to himself and crying. Several officers and paramedics ran for the backside of the building to see what they could do to help.

Tag moved past the police and headed closer to the building.

The next checkpoint wasn't manned by a police officer. This one had a man dressed in a suit, and Tag could only believe that he was a federal agent. This man didn't hold up a hand but stepped in the way of the opening. He gave off an air of authority, which instantly kicked in the military training Tag had received.

"You can't come in here."

"My pregnant wife is in there."

"I don't care if your pregnant grandmother is in there... You are not going past this barricade."

"You don't understand....

"I do understand, sir. You, like the other hundred or so people, have someone they love who was supposed to be inside this building. But if we let all of you past this barrier, then we will have a hundred people plus the ones already inside to take care of when the next bomb decides to blow."

"Is there another bomb?" A chill went through Tag's body. Did they know something? If another bomb went off, the entire building could fall in, structurally sound or not.

"I can help!" Tag yelled.

"How can you help, sir?"

"I'm a Marine...from EOD, the bomb unit. I was overseas for two tours and did exactly what you guys are trying to do."

"Are you still in the service?"

"No. I'm a civilian now."

"Right, a civilian." Someone must have called the man's name because he turned and talked to the person who was stepping closer. Once the man turned, Tag could see the back of his jacket said "FBI."

Turning around again, he said, "Please, let us handle it. We will try our best to get your wife out safely."

The FBI agent nodded at the man, who stepped up and then walked away. Tag was left standing along the barricade with the rest of the onlookers.

He pulled out his phone and dialed Grace's number again. He prayed she would pick up, and, when her voice came across, at first he thought she had. But as he listened to what turned out to be her voicemail message, Tag hoped this wouldn't be the only way he would ever hear her voice again. At least he was getting her voicemail. That was a plus — it meant the phone was working.

Suddenly, an explosion went off in Tag's head, and he went flat on the ground, ready to crawl forward. He had heard his buddy's voice cry for help!

I have to save him! He is only ten yards in front of me...Dear God, he's dead. Why? Why him and not me? I have to get to him. I have to! I can't stand it; I just can't take it anymore.

Tag's thoughts were slipping past common sense.

A policeman was talking to Tag. "Sir, get up off the ground. You have to stay behind the lines with the others. Crawling will not get you in!"

Tag realized what had happened. He had been transported back...again. He had to get his wits about him, or he wouldn't be able to save Grace and their baby.

He smiled at the officer as he stood on his feet. *God, I sure do need a drink....*

CHAPTER

TWELVE

"The other side isn't as damaged as this side seems to be." Jawad gave a look up to the ceiling and then back to Emil. "I think it might be better for everyone to be over there. Plus it is closer to bathrooms and the commissary."

"Sounds like a plan. At least the only one we have at the moment."

Grace noticed he was sizing up the people who were gathered in the area and stopped when he came to her. She had seen him before, when he'd had an altercation with the guard earlier. She felt he was analyzing her, maybe due to her pregnant size. It wasn't easy going through all this, while carrying a life inside you.

"By the way, my name is Jawad. And yes, I am a Muslim, and I don't care whether any of you like me or not."

He pointed at Grace and said, "I think she should go through first."

"I agree. And I'm Tommy." Tommy jumped up, shook Jawad's hand, and then helped Grace to her feet.

"Then Jerry has to come next! Promise me, Tommy! Jerry will be next!" Grace didn't want her friend left behind. Tommy nodded, so she allowed herself to be moved to the opening. It brought murmurs from the others.

Jawad said he would go through first in order to help people as they came through the debris on the other side. He cleared a few more pieces of rubble from the floor and then gave the all-clear for Grace to come through.

She squeezed her way into the opening rubbing her stomach a bit as she pushed herself through. Grace prayed that the pressure on her stomach wouldn't harm her baby.

Once she was on the other side, she helped as Jerry's body was moved through and then the small cart. With him back on it, Grace started helping the others in their party as they came through.

They introduced themselves to Jawad as they entered through the rubble. In the end there was Jerry,

Marta, her son Larry, Tommy, Emil and Jawad, as well as herself. A sound came from the other side of the room and they all hurried across, with Grace trailing behind since running wasn't an option at this stage in the pregnancy.

When she reached the already-gathered group, they discovered that another group had had the same idea and was coming through a hole they had made in the rubble from another area. The difference in this group was that most of them were severely wounded.

"Help!" It was a man from the other side trying to push a man through but was having a tough time.

Jawad and Emil grabbed the first man's arms and helped him get through the opening. He was obviously unconscious. Once they had him on the ground, Emil went to work trying to resuscitate him.

He started CPR. "Help better be arriving soon," he said as he went back to his efforts.

The others helped the rest of the people coming through, seven in all. Grace set to work getting people patched up, as best she could, while Marta and Larry watched.

Two had only a few cuts or scrapes, while others were in danger of losing organs. Two more were laid to the side of the room since they were already gone. Grace used more strips from her skirt to make bandages. She was thankful for the length and fullness of the skirt that made it possible to use a lot of material and still leave her decently dressed. There certainly wasn't anything else she could find.

Although pregnant, she didn't allow that to interfere with helping whenever she could. She needed to do something other than sit around. Once everyone was together again, they stood around in the center and watched as Emil continued to alternate between chest compressions and mouth-to-mouth. The group figured out what Emil obviously didn't want to believe.

"I think he's gone, Emil." Grace watched as Marta knelt beside him, putting her hand on his shoulders, which were still going up and down even though the man still hadn't responded.

"No. He can't be." Emil continued his CPR, but Grace could tell he was getting tired. He wasn't going to last much longer trying his best to bring this man back from where he obviously could not come back.

"Yes, he is." Marta placed her hand on top of his hands, still pumping on the man's chest. "You need to conserve your energy. You tried, but there is nothing anyone in here can do for him now. If you wear yourself out, what will happen if someone else needs your help?"

Emil slowed down and then finally stopped with the compression. He stayed on his knees beside the man, with his head hung down. Marta put her hand on the back of his neck.

Grace was impressed with Marta's efforts to offer what comfort she could. It didn't appear to be something she did frequently. At least she could be of some help.

Tommy helped Emil lay the dead man next to the other two who were already gone when they came through the hole.

Jawad looked around at the people and suddenly jumped up.

"Has anyone seen an older man? He walks with a cane. He helped me clear the debris for you guys and then went off for water, and I haven't seen him again."

The group shook their heads, all still focused on the three dead bodies and the two who didn't look like they would make it much longer.

It seemed to Grace like Emil had finally reached his acceptance with the man's death as he quickly stood up. "What the hell happened, man?" He turned toward Jawad.

CHAPTER

THIRTEEN

Emil turned to Jawad and wanted to know what was going on. Marta joined in with him.

What happened? Are they for real? Jawad was getting tired of being the one blamed. *I don't owe them any explanations!*

"I was heading across the building for my passport meeting when there were several explosions. Then, when I had finally gotten myself back up, there were a couple more. That is all I know."

The group started to mumble and look at Jawad. He wasn't stupid. He knew what was happening. They saw someone who was Muslim and instantly assumed he was the cause of this disaster.

Well, you got one thing right — we hate you stupid infidels. But I can't tell you that until I get home to my people!

This country talked about being a place for freedom, but since the attack on New York, there weren't many of the Muslim faith who were free. Not here, anyway. How he hated America, these people, and their god! *Allah is the only real God!*

"Why exactly are you in the building?" Marta took a step closer to Jawad.

"As I said, I had a meeting about my passport."

"Revoking it, I'll bet!" Larry was sarcastic in his tone. Marta smiled at her son.

"No. Actually it was going through." Jawad was seething inside.

He should have known from the moment that the explosion had happened that he would be the one getting the blame. Like killing infidels was a problem! If push comes to shove, he would defend himself without a second thought, and he was pretty sure they would not like what would happen then.

Jawad was tired of being bullied by the people in this country who claimed to be all about America. If things got worse, he wasn't going to cower in a corner. He would fight for his freedom, just like everyone else.

"Everyone needs to calm down," Grace got to her feet with the help of her friend Tommy. Jawad paid particular attention to what she was saying.

"We are going to be in here for a while. Nobody is coming into this building until it is known to be safe."

Jawad watched her look around at everyone. "We need to get water and make sure everyone is taken care of. Fighting among ourselves isn't going to help anyone."

The people reluctantly agreed and sat back down, along with Grace.

Jawad liked that lady. She was what Americans call "a real class act." Beautiful and classy, the perfect combination for a Muslim. Too independent for his tastes, however. *Too bad she isn't going to make it out alive.*

~ ~ ~

Seeing everyone settle down again, Grace felt a small amount of pride. She knew this was exactly how Tag would have handled the situation.

The thought of Tag sent a moment of sorrow through her system. Things hadn't been the best between them lately, and she knew she was partially to blame. Partially? Not understanding his problems, she was probably much more to blame than he was.

When I get out of here, she thought to herself, *I will make sure to be more supportive of him and help him through this tough time. This horror right here is what he had lived with every day for both tours.*

How could I not have seen the pain in his eyes and been more supportive? No wonder he turned to the bottle. It was the only friend he had, because I certainly had not been one. If I get out of this alive, I will be the wife he needs.

Lord, please forgive me, and let me make it up to him. He has suffered so much, and I have let him down. Get us out of here safe, and with You, I will help him heal.

~~~

"This is Marion Anderson, bringing you updates as we get them. The conditions at the scene haven't changed much. Firefighters and police are helping the last of the victims who have made their way out of the back of the building."

Marion stood in front of the camera, wearing the shortest skirt possible. She was glad she had gotten her hair done the night before, since she would be reporting the whole day on this story.

This was going to be her big chance to show the executives at the studio that she was more than legs and large breasts — not that those attributes weren't helpful to a career in TV.

"The FBI arrived roughly a half hour after the first three explosions and have been busy in the command center ever since. They have confirmed they believe this attack on an American government building is due to terrorists, however, no one has stepped forward to claim responsibility at this time."

She looked down at her notes and continued, "They believe there are people still alive and trapped inside the building, but as of now there does not appear to be rescue attempts being made. The authorities have advised that until they are sure there will be no further danger, they aren't sending any of their people into the building."

The camera moved to the people who were crowding around the barricades.

"People have been steadily filtering onto the scene since the first blasts. The authorities are urging everyone to stay away.

"If you believe a loved one was at the post office at the time, the number at the bottom of the screen will help you report their name as well as get updates. Again, please stay away from the scene at this time."

~ ~ ~

Tag stood off to the right of the reporter and shook his head. He could be in there helping these people instead of listening to this barely-out-of-school blonde talk into a camera. He'd had experience dealing with terrorists and their bombs. Why wouldn't they let him help?

He was appalled at what he heard next from the reporter.

"We do have one of the first civilians who responded to this disaster." The female turned toward a heavyset gentleman in his late forties. He was standing tall and proud as the camera panned to him. "What can you tell us about that first blast?"

"Well," the man placed his hand on the microphone. "I was heading toward the post office myself since I needed to get my taxes in the mail. I stopped because my shoe had come untied.

When I looked up, I saw a group of them standing by the side of the building. I had taken only two steps, and the place exploded."

"What do you mean by *'them'*?"

"You know. The ones who attacked New York."

The camera turned back to the young lady, who had a small smile on her face. "You've heard it here first. A witness spotted people of Middle-Eastern heritage snooping around the side of the building before the explosion.

"As a reminder, please stay away from the scene. Fire trucks and police cars have blocked all roads to the area.

"This is Marion Anderson. Back to the newsroom."

CHAPTER

FOURTEEN

Grace looked around the room and was in shock from all that had been happening. They got everyone patched up and helped the two most severely damaged men get bandaged and comfortable, although there were already three men who hadn't made it. The group of people seemed to naturally gravitate to the middle, where the central colonnade was. Besides Jerry, Marta, Larry, Tommy, Emil, Jawad, and herself, there were at least four other people all gathered together. Two of those still alive were in bad shape.

She had to admit — it felt safer being together. Grace was saddened that Marta and she were the only women found alive, at least that she knew of.

"I sent the older man for water right when I found your group," Jawad said as he pointed to Grace." For some reason, they all tended to talk to her as if she were in the position to make a decision. "He hasn't come back yet, and I'm afraid he might have gotten hurt. Maybe someone should go and look for him. He seemed like a nice old guy, willing to help."

The group made a sound of murmurs that Grace could only assume was speculation on whether Jawad might have had something to do with the missing gentleman — and the reason why he would want to leave what they considered the safest place to be.

"I think it is best from here on out if everyone stays together," Emil chimed in.

Grace got the impression Emil did not like the fact that she seemed to have been chosen the spokesperson and not him.

"I agree with him." Marta put her arm on Emil's shoulder, giving him one of her seductive smiles. Grace couldn't see her attracted to Emil's type, but stranger things had happened. She knew his attempts to save that man had ingratiated him to most of the people left alive.

"That sounds good," someone said. "But if for some reason you choose to leave and get lost or separated from the group, this could be the meeting place. Find your way back here. This could become the home base."

"What about water?" one of the people toward the side asked.

Grace didn't like where this conversation was going. The people were thinking about staying in this place until help arrived, which she knew wasn't going to be any time soon. Tag had told her what happened when a bomb went off, and she knew the search wouldn't begin until everyone was sure no more explosions would happen.

"I think what we need to do is start finding a way out." She didn't want to cause people to get hurt, but something needed to be done.

"No, no. We need to stay here. If we go running off throughout the building, we could get hurt or worse. This is safe, and they will come to rescue us."

Emil reminded Grace of a rooster with the way he puffed out his chest as he continued, "Who knows what shape the rest of the building is in?"

"I agree with him." Marta said, smiling up at him again.

Grace rolled her eyes at Marta. Since the incident with the man dying, all the woman had done was hang on Emil. But what she could see of him, he wasn't anyone they should be following.

She had known guys like him all of her life. They come across as if they wanted to take charge, but they always took the easiest and safest way out. She had seen Tag as different from the moment she'd met him.

Her attention was distracted by Jawad. Grace was surprised that he wasn't joining in the discussion. She watched him as the others debated on whether they should start to look for a way out or stay where they were.

He was looking around the room, taking everything in. Grace had not come to a conclusion about this man or if he'd had anything to do with the bombing, but he certainly wasn't acting scared, like the rest of them.

"I'm going to look for the old man." Jawad suddenly turned back to the group. "I feel responsible since I sent him after water. Plus, I can see if there is any food. Two birds with one stone."

Those words sent a chill through Grace's whole body. The baby felt it, too, giving a swift kick to her ribs. She gave a little huff and bent over. The group rushed to make sure she was okay.

"Kicking. The baby was just kicking." She righted herself and looked around. Jawad was gone, and the hair on the back of her neck stood up.

~~~

The few wounded found outside had been taken to a triage area about two blocks away from the bombing. The FBI also decided this needed to be the center of their operation since the other command center was too close to the building. They had certainly taken charge from the moment they'd arrived at the scene.

Tag was directed there after his tenth time of bugging the man who'd replaced the previous FBI agent. He made his way slowly, not sure if he wanted to see Grace there or not. He certainly didn't want anything to happen to her or the baby. If she was there, hopefully she wasn't too badly injured.

He stepped up to the table located right beside the tent opening. He could hear the moans of pain from the people inside. Some were crying, while others screamed in pain. Could Grace really be here? For a moment, he thought he would get sick.

"May I help you?" The nurse didn't look the least bit friendly.

Tag instantly felt they really needed to find someone better for this position. It is the only contact a lot of family members will have with their loved ones. They needed someone who was friendly and caring, not a no-nonsense nurse who had been working in medicine since before Tag was born.

"Yes, my wife was at the post office when the bomb went off. Grace Reynolds."

The woman looked through the pages of names. She checked it three times before looking back at him. "I'm sorry. Nobody by that name has been brought in. Can you give me a description? I will look for that."

"She's nine months pregnant. That should make her stand out."

"I know we don't have any pregnant women. Maybe she got out before the bombs exploded. Have you thought about trying to check your house?"

"She called me right before the first bomb went off. I know she was in there." Tag hadn't really thought those words until now. He felt sure he would be sick.

"I'm sure there are survivors in there. She will be fine." She reached across the table and patted his hand. "If you leave me a number, I will call if we get any news of a pregnant woman."

Tag felt bad for reading the woman wrongly. He didn't take into account the stress she must have been under, and he let her looks deceive him. He gave her his number, knowing she would be helpful to other families in distress.

He looked around the area, hoping to find someone he knew. There were men who'd come home from the war with him and eventually made their way into law enforcement, not really ready to give up the mission.

That was when he noticed the men dressed in bomb gear. The bomb squad had arrived. Maybe if they realized they had some ex-military help, then he could learn more about what is going on. He moved closer and heard them talking.

"We are holding off until we have more information," the one who looked to be in charge said.

One of the other men tried to argue, but all the man in charge had to do was give him a sour look for him to close his mouth. This wasn't going to work. Tag grabbed the nearest man dressed completely in protective gear.

"You need to send in a drone. That way you can see what damage there is and if there are any more bombs."

The man stopped and stared at Tag for a moment. "Who are you?"

"Tag Reynolds. I was on the bomb squad over in Iraq for two tours."

The man nodded his head and shrugged. "Three tours. Not bomb, though, until back here. You saw some pretty nasty stuff, no doubt."

"That I did."

"Lost a lot of my buddies over there." The short time they spoke took them temporarily back into the war.

"The worst was my best friend, Brian Peterson."

CHAPTER

FIFTEEN

Tag nodded his head at the police officer who had lost his best friend overseas, trying not to go into his past. He knew a lot of "Brians," but he couldn't remember a "Peterson." He hoped this cop was having an easier time at being a civilian than he was.

"You need to tell whoever is in charge to send in drones. They are perfect for this," Tag assured him.

The cop thought for a moment and then waved another man over and talked with him. They both would stop and look at Tag, raising his hopes that they might actually allow him to be involved in some way. After a few more words, the other man came over to where Tag was standing behind the barricade.

"You were in bomb overseas?"

"Yes, sir. Marines," Tag answered.

He nodded his head. "Good idea on the drones. But I need you to stay out of this. The FBI isn't going to want any military interfering until they are officially called in."

Tag nodded his head but was glad the man had actually listened to him. If it had been his squad dealing with this situation, the drones would have been in there already, and things would have been progressing.

The group of men in complete protective gear were gathered around a small table with a number of different monitors. The man he had connected with earlier made his way closer.

Tag was happy he wasn't made to head back behind the barricades. He watched from where he stood, making sure to stay out of everyone's way. Maybe once they had a look inside, they would let him get involved. He knew how to handle bombs made by terrorists.

His mind went straight to the last tour. Tag had been working with the group for more than a year when they came across a normal-looking house. They were doing routine checks and then discovered the bombs — not one, but seven in all — placed strategically around the building to make sure nothing and no one would survive the blasts.

Tag struggled for more than an hour to get every one of them deactivated. The next day, he discovered that enemy forces had re-entered the building and killed everyone in the family, including the baby he had gotten to hold once the bombs were deactivated the day before.

The father was rumored to be opposed to the local government and was helping the area soldiers. For that, everyone in his family was brutally eliminated. Holding that baby had made him decide to tell Grace he was ready to be a daddy the moment he had returned home.

Tag shook his head to clear the thoughts of those bodies he had stepped around the following day. He needed to focus on the best way he could help his wife get out of this situation. *Focus, Tag. FOCUS!*

The drone was set up and ready to be deployed. A young man was at the controls, and Tag was horrified. There's no way this kid would have the experience to handle that drone properly!

"Sir!" Tag was saying to anyone who would listen. "I have a lot of experience in handling drones. Maybe I should operate it."

"I'm not doubting your abilities, son, but I can't allow that. It would be my head if I let a civilian take charge and anything went wrong. Sorry, but I just can't let you do that. Stay back and watch, or I will have to have you removed."

There was a flurry of movement by the men around the table, and Tag took a closer look at the screen nearest to him. The drone was up and heading into the building. They were lucky to locate a hole that led into the parking garage underground. Customers didn't use it, but employees did, as well as delivery trucks.

A crystal-clear image of the destruction showed on the screen. Cars, parked by the employees at the beginning of what they believed was going to be a normal shift, had been smashed by huge pieces of concrete that had fallen from above.

Gas and oil was spreading across the floor from the engines. One little spark and everything would go up in flames. He could only imagine what the place smelled like. Still, if someone could get down there, they could escape through the garage ramps.

The man steering the drone was having a hard time keeping it steady. The image on the screen would go up and down and then suddenly zoom in a circle.

"Move to the left a little and then right. It will get you through that opening ahead." Tag said, casually, hoping the man would follow directions. And he did.

The drone reached another area, completely filled with rubble. It took Tag a few seconds to realize it had once been the elevator, taking people to the higher level of the post office. No bodies had been found yet, which gave Tag a small measure of hope.

"The opening to the left will be big enough for the drone." He nodded to the screen, watching the men around him. He took a few steps closer and pointed to the opening he was talking about.

"That doesn't look big enough," the young man driving the drone stated. He gave a quick look up to Tag.

"It will make it through — trust me."

The kid refused to listen to him this time and engineered the drone toward a hole at the top. The young man hit the walls a few times and even scraped along the ceiling. Tag was praying it would work out.

Suddenly everything went black for a moment, and Tag worried it was a dead end, but then the image returned, and everyone gave a sigh of relief. The drone did another loop, finally turning toward the opening.

Then everything went dark, and a loud crunch pierced through the speaker. The hole was not large enough for the drone to fit through.

"We lost it."

Angry, Tag took a step back to keep from telling off the superior officer who put human lives in the hands of an incompetent kid. This was their chance to finally get to the people in the building, and they'd blown it. The drone was gone, and it would be hours before they could get another one. *If* they could get another one.

He turned and walked away from the men who were still staring at the screen. He would need to find another way to get to his wife.

CHAPTER

SIXTEEN

Grace sat on the bench but knew she would soon need to get up and move around. Her back and hips were really starting to hurt. She hoped it was just from the sitting on the hard bench and not the injuries she felt in those areas — or the early arrival of her baby. Rubbing her back seemed to help but not enough to make her feel comfortable.

People were scattered in the big open area, sitting on the floor and talking. It seemed more like a camp meeting to Grace than people trapped in a bombed-out building. She guessed it could be worse with people crying and screaming. How she wanted to get out of this building and be with her husband!

"How did you end up here?" Marta sat down next to Grace. She wasn't sure if the woman really wanted to know or just wanted an excuse to share the bench. Everyone had given it to Grace, since she needed it more than they did; at least that was what Tommy had told them. And the group agreed.

"I actually had to drop off our taxes since we forgot to mail them last week." At this point, Grace knew it no longer mattered whose fault it was. She better understood why things were happening at home the way they were.

~ ~ ~

The pregnant woman — "Grace" was her name — had told her why she was at the post office, so Marta decided to talk. "I had a package to send." She hoped the woman next to her wouldn't ask what type of package.

Marta really wished she'd never agreed to go to the post office this morning for her boyfriend. She knew whatever was in the box wasn't legal, but she agreed anyway. That's when he insisted she bring along her kid. It was either that or end up in the emergency room again. She had been his punching bag for way too long.

One thing is for sure, Marta thought, *I am going to change my life when I get out of this mess. This whole experience has made me realize exposing my body to dirty old men — just so my boyfriend could live well — is a stupid thing to do. That druggie doesn't love me. He just needs me to make money for him.*

How could I have been so ignorant for so many years? Like it or not, it's over! Larry sure won't be sorry to see that bad-ass gone. Lord knows, my son has been as mistreated by Sam as I have. How could I have allowed that?

She was glad she wasn't in the same fix the other woman was. Being pregnant was the last thing she would ever want to be again. She had been sexually abused all her life and then having some gang-banger rape her at fourteen was just the exclamation point on that sentence.

Add to that, you find out you're going to have the rapist's kid. Well, that taught her to never get herself in that position again. The doc took care of that problem when her son was born. Never again.

~~~

"I, too, had to drop off a package. It was only supposed to take a minute. Boy, did I pick the wrong minute," Emil chimed in after Marta's statement. "What about you?" Emil turned and looked at Tommy.

"College scholarship papers. I needed to have them in the mail today to make next week's deadline." He looked around the room at all the debris lying around and said with a grin, "I don't think the papers are going to make it in time."

"I'm sure they will understand if you call them. You couldn't help that the post office decided to get blown up today." Grace hoped that, whatever happened, Tommy would be able to continue his schooling. She had grown quite fond of the young man who'd put himself in peril just to protect her and the baby. If the scholarship didn't work out, she would definitely be making some calls on his behalf.

"Isn't it funny how something so normal as going to the post office for a roll of stamps ends up with you being surrounded by strangers, praying for men in gear to come barging in?" someone in the back said.

Everyone laughed, and some continued the humor with comments like, "Hope that gear includes a burger and fries!"

"And some beer!"

"It does make you think about what is important in life." Grace knew this experience was going to change all of their lives in some way or another. It was certainly going to change the way she looked at her husband. She never could have imagined being in a situation like this.

When Tag would talk about the things he saw — which wasn't often — while he was overseas, she never imagined it looking like this. Now she understood why he was in such bad shape. There was death and destruction everywhere, and there was nothing she could do about it.

"When is your kid due?" Marta pointed at Grace's stomach like it was a thing, instead of a baby.

"My due date is next Tuesday."

"Are you scared?" That comment got everyone's attention, as they quietly waited for a response.

Grace grinned at the woman and then at the people around her. "After being trapped in a bombed-out post office? Piece of cake."

The group let out another moment of laughter. It was a brief relief, but much needed. For a while, each told a story of how they found themselves at the post office that day.

Some even went on to tell how this tragedy had altered their thinking and how they were going to make changes in their lives when this was over. Grace was amazed at how such a tragedy could actually create some positive results.

"I can't believe I was actually mad at my wife a couple hours ago. For what? She didn't have time to pick out my clothes for me this morning before leaving for work! Can you believe that? Now all I want to do is hold her in my arms." A nice-looking man in the back was shaking his head at the stupidity of it all.

Grace couldn't help but add, "It certainly gives you a new perspective, doesn't it?"

They all answered, "Amen!" "No kidding." "Right!"

One said he was going to spend more time with his children. He went on to say that if he had died in this disaster, they wouldn't have very many memories of him. He was going to change that. Another man said, "Me, too!"

Another said he had been avoiding making a commitment to his girlfriend, but this event had caused him to realize he really loved her and wanted to grow old with her. He also said it had taught him that if he didn't do something now, there may not be a tomorrow. Everyone had to agree with that.

A couple more comments made Grace say a quiet prayer, thanking God for the wonderful, positive things that were coming out of such a tragedy.

Marta still seemed interested in Grace's baby. "Did you get an ultra-thingy?"

Grace wanted to laugh but didn't.

"An ultrasound? Yes, one was done, but they never showed it to my husband or me, because we didn't want to know the sex of the baby. We just wanted to be surprised by whatever God gave us. The ultrasound was done to make sure everything was okay with him."

Then Grace quickly added, "I say 'him' because I'm sure it's a boy."

"How do you know?" Marta asked the obvious question.

One of the men in the back said, "Don't ask! A woman just knows. How, I have no idea, but they know!"

More laughter to release tension.

"I never had an ultrasound when I was carrying Larry. I was pretty poor then and never got any prenatal care. I don't want more kids. One's enough."

"I don't want any at all." Emil was firm in his belief.

"Why not?" Grace was always curious why people didn't want children in their lives. A couple of her friends felt the same way, yet they had done nothing but check on the baby since they found out Grace was pregnant.

They were also responsible for rounding up about seventy percent of the used baby clothes she had.

"I didn't have a great childhood."

"Neither did I, but that isn't a reason not to have a family of your own. You just do your best to make their childhood better than the one you had."

"Believe me, my childhood was beyond what normal people would consider bad." The group watched as Emil hung his head in thought. Then he took a deep breath.

"We were poor. I mean no money at all, poor. We lived on the street and ate at shelters. My mother and father tried really hard for my four siblings and me. And it was surprising they stayed together through it all. But then..." He started to choke up.

"Then some drug dealer decided our living on the street was getting in the way of his business. He walked right up to our little area one night and just started shooting. Luckily, I was in the far corner, and he didn't see me, but I was the *only* one he didn't see," Emil took a deep breath before continuing.

"I ended up in foster care and made a vow never to have children. Children shouldn't be brought into this world the way it is." He looked at Grace and then continued.

"I never wanted kids. I married a woman who knew how I felt, and she said she felt the same way. But then last year, she ran off with some white dude who works at this very post office, and now that trash is pregnant. No offense, ma'am. Sometimes at night, I lie awake thinking of ways to pay them back for what they have done to me."

"But at least your parents were together through it all. They must have really loved each other. That is more than most of us can say," Marta said directly to Emil.

"My father left when I was ten. One night my mother caught him raping me again. It actually started when I was six, but he didn't get caught until I was ten. She went after him with a butcher knife, but he got it away from her.

"The next day, he decided to beat the living shit out of my mother for threatening him — and then my younger brother and me just for fun. He then ran off and disappeared.

"We were all in the hospital for more a week recovering. But through it all, my mother never once said a bad word about him. I would beg her. I would plead for her to tell the cops who'd hurt us, but she refused."

"Did you tell?" Grace placed a hand over Marta's.

"I couldn't. Mom made me promise, and one thing I have never done was break a promise. Believe me, when the cops kept asking who was raping me, I wanted to tell them. Boy did I want to. But, I also believed that if I did, he would come back and finish what he'd started. The cops kept asking where the man of the house was, so I know he got put on their radar."

"What happened to your father?" Tommy asked quietly.

"He was killed in prison after he beat up the second family he had. They say prisoners don't like child abusers, and, apparently, they are right."

You could tell Marta was pleased with the outcome. She waited a minute before going on.

"After all these years, I found a guy I thought loved me, but he doesn't. He is just using me, but I am going to change that." She then put her arm around her son, who looked happy at her statement.

"What about you, Tommy?"

CHAPTER

SEVENTEEN

Tommy looked around at the group, was thoughtful for a moment, and then started.

"Well, my family was *great*. We were fairly well off and lived in a nice house with a swimming pool. They encouraged me to get into sports, and the whole family came to all my football games. They would allow me to have parties on the weekends.

"Dad would arrange pool-party cook-outs for my friends. I was the most popular kid in school because of my parents. You know, the type of parents all children dreamed of having. And I *thought* I had it pretty good." Tommy stopped there.

"*'Thought'* you had it good? I don't get it. Sounds like what heaven is supposed to be like to me." Emil frowned at Tommy's remark.

"You're right, Emil. I *did* have it good, very good. At least until I was seventeen. That's when I finally told them I was gay." Tommy didn't seem to have a problem letting everyone know.

You could hear the gasps. They all stopped and looked at Tommy.

"Yep. I'm gay. Something not many people talk about in groups of strangers. I guess that was why the news was such a shock to my family.

But it doesn't explain, at least to *me*, why they kicked me out of the house, onto the street, and told me never to come back." Tommy's pain showed on his face. "I now work two jobs to rent a room and put myself through college."

Grace reached her hand out to her friend. She was surprised he'd been so truthful, but there was no reason he shouldn't have been. He had fast become a dear friend.

She jumped in to prevent any negative comments. "Well, that really doesn't matter, does it? You have been nothing but caring in *my* hour of need. You also must be very dedicated to work all those hours, go to school, and study on top of that! I'll bet you will be a CEO someday. We'll be able to say we knew you back when you preferred bombed-out buildings!"

Tommy's grateful glance was heartwarming, and the others laughed at her joke.

Someone said, "Yeah, we all have a soft spot for hot ashes."

Tommy's big grin was followed with, "What, you don't like my latest Ash Clothing Collection? Silly people!" He waved his hands to display the dirty shirt he had on. "You, too, can have one of these priceless garments, on sale today — just for *you!*" He pointed his finger in their direction.

"No thanks. I already have one!"

"On sale? As in 'giveaway'?"

"'Just for us' — riiiiiight! Where have we heard that one before?"

Another hollered, "I can attest to it being a wonderful collection! Look at this ash jacket I'm wearing! And now bombs will always be on my Christmas list. And I don't have to buy coal for stockings anymore. We can use chunks of cement!"

The laughter continued for several minutes and helped take the edge off.

The group broke up and started on their own conversations after a few more shared why they did and didn't want to have children.

Marta went to sit beside Emil, apparently to talk more about their childhoods. Tommy sat down beside Grace.

"Thanks," he said quietly, with admiration in his eyes.

"My pleasure," Grace pushed her shoulder into his. Leaning toward Tommy, she added, "But I meant what I said. It really doesn't matter. That's between you and God, not any of us here."

Grace saw Tommy look at Jerry and sadly shake his head. She knew Jerry was dead, but nothing was going to make her leave him here in this horrible place. She was getting out, and so was her friend.

She wanted to give his parents the chance to give him a wonderful funeral. It was the least she could do. That is, if *she* got out alive.

She couldn't shake something Emil had said. His wife had run off with a man who worked at *this* post office, and he wanted revenge...

Her thoughts were interrupted when Tommy handed Grace back her phone and she stared at it. She actually had a signal.

Wait! She had a *SIGNAL!*

She went through her contacts and pulled up Tag's number. She was just about to push his name when a pile of rocks suddenly came crumbling into the room from a pile against the wall, causing screams and scrambling.

Tommy was the first one to step in front of Grace. She wasn't sure what he thought his body would do for a pile of falling rocks, but she appreciated the effort. Then they heard a noise.

Emil and two other men walked over to the pile and leaned in.

"There's a guy on the other side."

The gang joined together and helped Emil move rock after rock until the opening was big enough for an older gentleman to be helped through. He had cuts and scratches on his head and hands, but he was carrying jugs of water with one hand and a cane in the other. His clothes were covered in blood.

"I wasn't sure if I would ever find people again." He set the jugs on the ground and started brushing and straightening his clothes. It was obvious he didn't like to be dirty or disheveled. But it was also pretty obvious there wasn't anything any of them could do about how they looked.

"Hi, my name is Fred. I came across a Muslim boy who suggested I go look for water. Took me a lot longer than I thought it would! How is everyone?" He seemed to scrutinize each person; he turned to the person closest to him, who happened to be Emil.

"Where is the Muslim boy?"

"I assume he went looking for you. He kept talking about an older gentleman who went after water." Emil's facial expressions made it clear he liked this old guy.

"I think he went to set up another bomb." Marta was the one talking now. "He and his kind are probably all hidden in this building, just waiting to set off another one. People like him can't be trusted."

Fred raised his eyebrows in shock, but some of the others nodded in agreement.

"I have an idea. My phone actually has a signal. Why doesn't everyone check their phones?" Grace needed to defuse this situation quickly.

If Marta was allowed to keep talking, who knows what kind of mob might have formed? The last thing they needed was a lynching. And in her heart, she wasn't ready to believe Jawad was responsible for what they were going through. Maybe he was, but now was not the time to make a judgment. Getting out of here alive was more important than anything else.

What if no one in her group was the bad guy? Everyone was trying to place blame, but the people responsible may have been long gone, celebrating the disaster they'd made out of so many lives.

After scrambling for their phones, they quickly discovered that only the phones belonging to Marta and Grace were still working. Everyone else's had been lost or too damaged. People lined up to use Marta's phone.

Tommy, Emil, and Fred stayed with Grace. Larry sat down against the far wall to take a nap. He wasn't interested in anyone's phone at all.

"Fred, is there anyone you want to call?" Grace didn't want it to appear that her calls were the only important ones. She knew that wasn't the truth, and Fred *was* the oldest.

"Uh, no, ma'am. My wife passed some time back. It's just me now. I don't think anyone out there cares if I am in here or not." With that, Fred stepped away from them.

Grace's heart sank at the pain in his eyes. Tommy and Emil both stated there was no one else to call and urged her to let her husband know she was okay.

As she pushed the call button, she was reeling with the thought that she was the only one who had anyone out in the world who cared whether she lived or died.

~~~

Tag took a few deep breaths, trying to keep the panic from welling up inside. He needed to get into that building. If no one else was going to go in, then he would. The longer they were in there, the greater the chance was of something happening to Grace and his child. He wasn't going to allow that to happen. Tag couldn't — *wouldn't* — entertain thoughts of Grace already being gone.

He had been in disastrous situations like this before, but most of the men in charge of this mess had never been. He had to pack up his fears and get on with the rescue.

He moved along the left side of the building. He searched each opening, only to find one dead end after another. He had taken a few more steps when a hand landed on his shoulder.

"Excuse me, sir. But exactly what are you doing?"

"I need to get in there. My pregnant wife is inside."

"I understand that, but you can't go in. There are professionals taking care of it."

Professionals? Tag wanted to laugh in the man's face, but he knew that it would only cause the situation to get worse. He followed the man back to the barricade. He wasn't going to give up just because he had been caught. His determination was just as strong as his anger.

Once the officer was out of sight, Tag headed toward the right. He made it to the end of the barricade and watched as the policeman walked back and forth. All he needed was a distraction — the kind that would keep them from seeing him when he ran across the yard.

The screaming of an older African-American woman came right on cue. Tag could hear her screaming about her son being in the building. The officers headed in her direction the moment she started to move a barrier.

This was the chance he needed. Without thinking it through, he ran toward the right side of the building. He ducked behind a tree when one officer turned in his direction.

After a few more moments, there was another burst from the same woman. Once again, she had everyone's attention. Tag took off and reached the right side, where the officers could no longer see him.

He had just reached the corner to go around to the back when the world exploded. Three times.

(((BOOOOOM))))((BOOOOM))((BOOOOM))

The ground trembled under his feet, and pain filled his ears. The sixth, seventh, and eighth bombs had just gone off! One was really close, but the other two were located further away in the building.

The last one sounded like it was two blocks away! Not that they weren't taking down the same massive building, but it put the size of this attack in further perspective for him.

The building beside Tag shook, and pieces of the exterior started to crumble down onto his head. He headed for the cover of the trees.

He watched as the people around the barricade scrambled as more pieces fell. Although they were far enough back to keep from getting hit, the commotion caused the people to move further back on their own. Tag now expected that the barricades would be pushed back even farther from the building than they already were.

He was trying to come up with his next move when the phone in his pocket started to go off. Not with just any ring tone, but the one that Grace had set for herself — the song from their wedding!

As quickly as he could, he dug into his pocket to get the phone. He almost dropped it but got a firm grasp at the last second. He slid the bar over to connect the call.

"Grace?"

"Tag....fine....baby.....fine...I'm......... scared......Jer.....sorry.......love...."

"Grace. You're breaking up."

"Five.... Plea......"

The phone went silent. He looked at the object sitting in his hand, and it didn't register at first that his connection was lost. When it did, a part of him felt like he had lost Grace.

A tear formed in his eye, but then the words she said finally hit his brain. *She and the baby are fine, but she's scared. And she loves me. I have no idea what the chair or sorry was about, but I'll worry about that later.*

Now, all he needed to deal with was finally getting the bomb squad to listen to what he had to say. *Grace is alive! She's really alive!* was all he could think about.

People were still trapped, and he was betting that "five" was the number Grace knew to be alive. Being that close to the building actually was a good thing because this time he had information they needed. He now knew the type of bombs that were being used.

Through his years over in Iraq, he had heard and felt a number of different bombs explode. Each type had a different method of exploding and a different sound.

The closest one that just went off was cheap, and the parts to make it were readily available to most people. Tag no longer felt this was a terrorist action. Even a kid could make the bomb that had just gone off!

CHAPTER

EIGHTEEN

The new bombs had caught the group milling around the large area and chatting about family. Across the room, one man was even next to Marta using her phone.

As usual, ear-splitting noise brought fire, flying debris, and dust that was blinding.

Leaning over Jerry to protect his body from being hit, Grace could hear the crumbling of the walls. Once the noise settled down and she finally moved, she discovered that Emil and Tommy had both been shielding her from the falling debris. She was grateful and thanked them quietly. Tommy patted Emil on the back for his added help. Emil looked like no one had ever appreciated him before, and his chest pushed out as he smiled at them both.

Then they looked around at what used to be a large room.

The area where they had been five minutes ago was nothing but rubble, bringing part of the wall down with it. When she looked up, the ceiling of the colonnade was cracking, and pieces had begun to tumble to the ground.

As they were able to see their way around, they moved slowing, stepping over anything that didn't move. They found the bodies of people they had just been talking to.

Marta and the man using her phone appeared to be closest to the explosion. Her long bleached-blond hair was about all that was left to identify her by. Emil stood and looked at the bloody, mangled hair for a long time, while Grace and Tommy checked each person, in case they were only unconscious, but the body count kept mounting.

Not far from Marta, they found Fred, face down in the rubble. Grace started to cry. *No one cared if he was in here or not. Now no one will care that he's dead.* Tommy seemed to understand and put his arm around her.

Grace now had the only working cell phone. Marta's son, Larry, was standing by the wall, crying. She slipped from Tommy's arm and went to him. She held him tight as both their hearts broke.

They weren't going to find safe shelter for much longer in this area. Pieces continued to fall even now.

A commotion from the commissary area grabbed her attention. Jawad hurried into the open area, carrying four plastic bags.

"I came back as soon as I heard the last bombs! *RAEIB!* This place is...!" Jawad looked at the damage.

"I brought some food. It isn't much, but it should tide us over." He noticed that the room got suddenly quiet. "I wasn't able to find the older....."

"He was here. His name was Fred. He brought water like you asked." Emil stepped out from behind Tommy. He pointed to where Fred's body lay. "He didn't make it through the last blasts."

"Exactly where were *you?*" Larry's face was angry now. Grace could tell he was stretched about as far as a boy could go before losing it.

"I was looking for the older gentleman, Fred, and when I couldn't find him, I started looking for food." He held up the bag for proof. "Plus, I discovered an area closer to the back that doesn't have *any* damage. I think we should go there quickly and wait for help."

"Farther away? *Really?*" Larry was on the brink of exploding.

"You put us *here*, and look what happened! My Mom is DEAD!" Larry was screaming and crying at the same time.

"Look!" Grace put her arms around the boy. "There are only a few of us left alive that we know of. Fred told us the same story Jawad did, so there is nothing more to say. We will not argue. NOT! *Got it?*

"Further, we are not a bunch of sheep and do not have to follow anyone. We have to make up our *own* minds what we think is best for *us!* You can go anywhere you like or you can try to find a way out. That's up to each one of us."

"We have to do something. These walls aren't going to last long, so make up your minds," Tommy interjected.

It was then that the first real contraction hit Grace.

~~~

The blonde in the short skirt was standing in front of the television camera again. She loved her job, and today was certainly no exception. She was getting her face on the air more today than she had in the prior six months she had been working for the station.

"Right place. Right time."

"What?" The cameraman turned toward her.

"Nothing."

"We are on in three, two, one..."

"This is Marion Anderson, giving you updated reports on the Dallas Post Office bombing." She looked into the camera. A seriousness that the managers of the station hadn't seen before came across her face.

"As you can see behind me, there has been a *third* bombing, with three more bombs going off, one after another. They all exploded just a short while ago.

"At this time, it is becoming more and more doubtful there may be survivors, but authorities said they are not giving up yet." She turned toward the building to indicate for the cameraman to focus on the destruction.

"I spoke to the FBI right before coming on the air, and they said no terrorist group has come forward to claim responsibility."

She turned back to the camera, and the operator followed.

"The FBI is still trying to gather information as well as help any victims who are able to make their way out of the building, though none have as yet. When I continued to question the FBI spokesperson about why a team hadn't yet entered the building, the only reply he gave was "'No comment.'"

Anderson looked up and saw a man running at full speed toward the area barricaded for the FBI and bomb squad. Without thinking, she reached out her hand and pushed the microphone out in front of him. She thought to herself, *Hopefully, this is one of the people who had access to the tent and not another crackpot who had theories about why this was happening.*

"Excuse me. Are you with the FBI or bomb squad?"

"No," Tag said. "But my pregnant wife is inside, and I just spoke with her on my phone." He held it up, almost as if it would help make his point.

"You did?" She quickly moved closer to him and nodded for the cameraman to take her lead. "What is your name?"

"Tag Reynolds."

"What do you know about this tragedy?"

"Well, as I said, my wife, Grace, is nine months pregnant and trapped inside the building. She called right after the eighth bomb went off. I didn't have a clear signal, but I got that she was okay but scared."

"What about your baby?"

"She said that the baby is fine, also. At least for now."

"Have the authorities told you anything about what their plans are?"

"No, but I served two tours over in Iraq in the bomb unit. And I can tell you that the last explosions came from some type of pipe bomb."

"Really! A pipe bomb? How do you know that?"

"The sound. Now, if you will excuse me." Tag turned to walk away, but Anderson put her hand on his arm.

"What are you going to do now?"

"I'm going to save my wife and child!"

With that comment by Tag, Anderson watched him resume his run all the way to where the bomb squad was meeting.

The reporting that Anderson was doing from the scene wasn't being watched only by the people of Dallas. The segment that Tag had just appeared on was being broadcast across the United States and Canada. Facebook and Twitter lit up with his story, and it went viral within minutes. Anderson was informed through her earpiece that Tag was an instant hero.

People from all over were calling into the television station and talking about what a great man he was for trying to save his wife and unborn child, when no one else was doing anything to help those who were trapped!

Anderson's mind went into overdrive. *I need to keep a close watch on that man. 'Tag' was his name? He is just what I need to make me famous! My interview with him has already gone bananas on the Internet! Go figure! Wow! Life is good.*

~~~

Grace had kept the contraction to herself, although she wasn't exactly sure how she managed it. The last thing she wanted was everyone to panic about her going into labor.

She also took into consideration how upset everyone was getting about Jawad's suggestion. And who knows? It might have been one of those Braxton-Hicks things that the doctor had warned her about. The pain wasn't too bad. Her main concern right now was making her way to the undamaged area that Jawad had talked about.

She also wasn't too concerned about Larry at this time, as he was clinging to Emil. The two seemed to hit it off. Grace thought it was odd, considering Emil didn't want kids.

They all finally decided to go along with Jawad. It took a bit of discussion, but, in the end, when a big piece of the ceiling came crashing down into the middle of the clearing, it wasn't that hard of a decision to make.

The men worked together to clear a path. It took them a little while but not as long as Grace expected. While they worked, she kept looking over where

Fred lay. How sad he looked lying there alone.

Once the group started moving through the opening, everything went pretty smoothly. For once, there was no grumbling about taking Jerry. They just planned on it.

Once they reached the south side of the building, she was surprised by how minimal the damage really was. Jawad was right. The bombs must have been located closer to the other side. The exits were still blocked by concrete debris, but the ceiling looked to be in good shape.

They reached the offices where people went to get their passports. There were a number of desks and filing cabinets, but the area seemed almost untouched by the bombings. This was a relief for Grace since she felt another contraction as they crossed into the rooms.

Emil left to go to the bathroom. Jawad and Tommy gathered chairs for everyone to sit on in the center of the room, and Grace hovered over Jerry, making sure he had not sustained any more damage. She knew it was stupid, but she just wasn't ready to let go. Not yet. She rolled his cart up next to her chair and sat down to rest.

The next contraction was a little rougher than the previous one but still not terrible. It made her double over, but she didn't think the others had noticed.

"What happened on the way here?" Jawad stepped next to her. They hadn't talked a great deal before he had taken off earlier, but he had checked on her and the baby.

"Nothing."

"That was nothing? The look on your face alone..."

"I'm having those pretend contractions."

CHAPTER

NINETEEN

"'Pretend contractions'? Who would pretend to have contractions?" Jawad's face scrunched up in confusion, and it was obvious he had never heard the term before. Tommy was now standing close to him.

"They are known as Braxton-Hicks contractions. Women get them before birth — false labor. They can be brought on by stress."

"Not like you have any of that!" Jawad gave a little laugh, and Grace joined in. He had to admit these two people seemed to be okay in his book. Why couldn't all Americans be like them?

"Not at all. Just a normal day in the life of a pregnant woman."

"Okay." Jawad looked around at Tommy. "I just wanted to make sure you two were okay."

Grace appreciated him checking on her. In other situations, people normally wouldn't even notice the pregnant woman in the room, but everyone had made it a point to check on her since the first explosion. Maybe they thought the idea of having a pregnant woman inside would push the people outside to find them quicker, but she knew it wouldn't make any difference. The only person outside who was worried about her was Tag.

They created a type of junk-food buffet along one wall. Emil had returned, and the five of them grabbed something to eat. This was the first time since the bombs started going off that Grace actually felt safe. This was good, because another contraction ripped through her body. This time, it wasn't the least bit tame.

She wasn't surprised when Tommy noticed.

"What's wrong?" He placed a gentle hand on her shoulder.

"Nothing."

"You had another one of those Bratton-Higgins things again?" Jawad was right beside him.

"Yeah." She tried to brush off the pain and put a smile on her face, but this time she wasn't so sure that it was only a pretend contraction.

"I will tell you what is wrong with America today," Larry started, with his voice loud and using his hand to express his unhappiness. "It is all the policies that our government makes. Allowing people from other countries into ours is just asking for trouble."

The others got quiet, and Larry, still enraged by his mother's death, continued to yell and holler about immigrants and how if America had not allowed immigrants into the country back then, September 11th would have never happened. He turned to Jawad. His disgust for Muslims was obvious.

"And you!" His finger almost touched Jawad, and neither man was going to back down. "You... Don't think we didn't notice that you discovered the exact place you were supposed to be when the bomb went off. It is in a lot better shape than anywhere else. You want to explain that?"

Jawad sized up those around him to see if everyone believed the same thing.

"People like you are the reason this country lives in terror," Larry's voice was loud now. Emil stood beside him but didn't even try to interfere.

"You and your beliefs! We haven't done anything but help you people." With those last words, Larry almost spit into Jawad's face.

"My *beliefs?* You don't have any idea what my beliefs are! If you did, you wouldn't be standing here talking like some idiot. You would understand that just because people with the same beliefs did some horrendous things, that doesn't mean we are all the same."

Jawad couldn't take this kid yelling anymore, especially when he got into his face. The problem was that the angrier he got, the stronger his accent became, making him stand out even more.

"Your people killed innocent people for no reason other than hating Americans. In my book, you are all the same." Larry wasn't going to let go.

"Then I guess you are a killer, also."

"What?" Larry's face got hard as he stared at Jawad. "What are you implying?"

"What I'm saying is that your religion had its fair share of murderers, so that means, by your own reasoning, that you are also a killer since it is your religion."

"I'm Catholic," he said sarcastically.

"Even better... you're a killer *and* a child molester, like your priests."

That was the end for Larry. He pulled back his fist and attempted to slam it into Jawad's face. Jawad was ready and stopped the fist with his hand. Both stared with hatred at each other.

"Whoa! I think we need our separate corners." Emil stepped in between the two, placing a hand on each of their chests.

Larry was still angry but nodded his head. He turned and headed in the opposite direction.

Jawad headed to the table and starting sorting through the food that he had found, taking deep breaths in hopes of calming himself down.

That punk kid was the exact reason that so many of my fellow Muslims are miserable in this country.

"But isn't it kind of ironic that he was safely here when that bomb went off?" Larry just had to have the last word.

Tommy was the one to stand this time. "But so were the rest of us. And Jawad has done nothing but save us. He brought us together and then went off looking for Fred. Plus he found us food and this place. Someone who wanted to kill us would hardly have bothered to do that."

Emil was angry and shouted, "Everyone — just stop arguing! It will do no good, and it will not change anything. Remarkably, we're still alive after all the bombs. We could all be dead in a split second, so why is this crap about beliefs important?" He just shook his head and went to sit down.

Grace smiled at Emil. How different his attitude had become from earlier in the day. Tragedy will do that to people.

She was also very proud of Tommy. She wanted to jump up and hug him. Tommy was a fine man, and she was so glad she'd had the chance to meet him. She just wished it had been under better circumstances. But then again, if it had been under different circumstances, she would not have had the opportunity to see what a good man he was under pressure.

"Besides," Grace added, "what makes you think the person — or persons — responsible for this tragedy is here in our tiny group? Seriously? Can you justify that someone who wanted to bomb a government building would still be here?"

That remark brought silence to everyone. Emil was deep in thought, as was Jawad. Larry just shook his head.

"I'm going into the other room," Grace quietly said to Tommy. He nodded his head and helped her. He took one of the bottles of water with him. And just as they entered the room another blast of pain ripped through her stomach, and she knew this time it wasn't "pretend."

She was going into labor.

Tommy walked her across the room, sat her down at a desk, went back and rolled Jerry into the same room, and then shut the door. The three talking outside didn't even notice.

"You're having the baby." It was a statement, not a question. Tommy poured some water for Grace in the small paper cups he'd found in the bathrooms.

She drank down the water and nodded her head. She needed to get a hold of Tag and get out of this mess, so she reached for her phone. She and the baby were running out of time.

CHAPTER

TWENTY

The scene at the command center had turned into a circus since the last explosion. Tag attempted to get to the bomb squad in the hopes of sharing the information he knew about the bombs. But every attempt failed. Some policeman, firefighter, or FBI agent would spot Tag and send him away. And with some, the fact that he had been a Marine only made them more adamant.

He was trying again when his phone played Grace's song. Yanking it out of his pocket, he let out a little prayer that this time he would be able to talk to her without too much static. And, thankfully, the call was clear.

"Grace?"

"Tag?"

"Are you okay? And the baby?"

"Yes, the baby and I are okay." She couldn't tell him about the contractions. It wouldn't make anything better and would only cause him to worry more. "We found a place on the south side of the building that seems to be safe. What is going on outside?"

"They won't come in until they know it is safe. And the drone they were using got smashed. The last I knew they were working on getting another one, but don't count on that happening any time soon. What about where you are?"

"A few people are getting irritable, trying to throw blame." She took a deep breath. "Tag, there were so many dead bodies, especially after the last blasts. There are only five of us left in our little group. There may be others trapped elsewhere, but we have been to most parts of the building, so I doubt it. I'm scared." The tears flowed down her face.

"I know, honey." He wished he could pull her into his arms as a tear slid down his cheek. He hated the thought of only five people survivoring. The death toll from this event was mind boggling, and he couldn't wrap his mind around it.

"There is this kid who is at his breaking point. Larry something... He just picked a fight with a Middle-Eastern man, Jawad, accusing him of the attack. What we don't need is fighting among ourselves."

~~~

Tag let out a gasp at Jawad's name. "There is no proof that terrorists are responsible. But be careful anyway."

As Tag was trying to hear what his wife was saying, he was interrupted.

"Can we talk to you?"

"I'm on the phone with my wife right now."

The reporter urged the cameraman over with her hand. "Record this." Tag turned to her as she took the microphone, holding the phone close. Grace was able to hear what was being said.

"We are standing here with Tag Reynolds, the man we talked with earlier who told us what types of bombs are being used. And he now is talking to his pregnant wife on the phone, who is one of the people still trapped in the building. Can you tell us anything from inside the building, Mrs. Reynolds?"

"She says there are arguments among them about who is responsible. Lots of dead bodies. But they believe they have found a safe place."

"Tag?" Grace's voice came through the phone.

"Sorry, honey. Reporters are here and wanted to know anything they could from you."

"Tell them there are four people with me, and we are beat up pretty bad but safe," Grace said.

Tag relayed this information to the reporter and then turned and walked away so he could talk to his wife. He was pleased to see the reporter back off and give him some privacy.

Turning back to his wife on the phone, he said, "Listen, honey, you need to find a way to get out of the building."

"But Tag...."

"It's important. They aren't coming in any time soon. The last blasts just confirmed to them that the note they received about 'chaos times ten' was meant for this disaster. That means there are two more bombs that haven't gone off. I think if you can find your way into the basement parking garage, you will be able to get out. The drone got that far and the openings were plenty big enough for people. At least they were at the time."

"Okay."

"Honey, I know this is scary, but you must do this. *Please,* honey, just do as I say..." The phone started to break up. "And yes, Grace, the person responsible might still be in the building. We don't know what kind of pervert is responsible. It might not be terrorists." The phone went off and on a few times. "I love you."

He wasn't sure if his last message had gotten through or not. He hoped so. For Grace to know that he loved her more than his own life was the most important thing to him right now.

~~~

Grace just looked at the phone in her hand. The last words she heard was

Tag telling her that he loved her before the phone cut off. It was the first time in several months that he had said it. She felt like he had just proposed all over again. A single tear ran down her cheek.

With a quick flip of her hand, the tear was gone, and she knew what she needed to do. She was the only one able to get a call through to the outside, and her husband said they needed to get to the underground garage, not wait for help to come to them. And with the help of God, that is exactly what they were going to do! She would go alone if she had to.

Motioning for Tommy to sit down near her, she said, "Tommy, Tag said to get to the underground garage. He said there were openings where we could get out. I know you don't know him, but I believe he is right, and we need to get there as soon as...

Loud voices were coming through the shut door. Worried glances passed between them, as Tommy got up to cross the room and open the door.

Jawad was pushing Larry away, and everyone was yelling.

"I told you to stay away from me. I don't want any foreigners touching me, you hear?" Larry was near hysterics. Emil tried to calm him down.

Jawad moved to the other side of the room to get away from the anger.

"We are all a little testy right now." Emil stated, to no one in particular.

It was Tommy who spoke next, "Guys, we have a woman in labor here. Can we deal with the macho crap later?"

When all was quiet, another strong contraction hit her, and she cried out in pain. The three men ran into the room and stared at her. Tommy shut the door behind them as they all gathered around her.

Speaking now between puffs of air, Grace said, "Tommy, Jerry, and I are leaving this area. My husband said to get down into the basement, and that is what we are going to do. You can come or not. I don't care. I just know I am about to give birth, and I am not going to do it here."

They were all quiet for a moment, and then everyone agreed to go downstairs. Emil told anyone who would listen that he didn't understand why they had to leave a perfectly safe area, but who was he to argue...

Jawad was still leaning on Fred's cane, but he was able to walk fairly well. Not so much for Grace. She was having a difficult time. She had to lean on Tommy and stop frequently for the pain. But the real problem was rolling the cart along with Jerry on it.

"Look, lady, I understand your wanting to see that your friend gets a proper burial and all that. I really do, but I don't want to die trying to help a dead man get out of here." Emil was watching Tommy trying to move the cart Jerry was lying on and assist Grace, too.

"You can have him removed tomorrow or whenever, but you are so adamant about our getting ourselves out of here that it seems crazy to drag..."

"*JERRY IS GOING WITH ME!* You — nor anyone else — has to like it! You don't have to go if you don't want to. That's it. There isn't any other option. Jerry is going with me! *Got it?*" Grace had gone through about as much as she could bear.

Her patience had worn thin with everyone and everything. The bombs, the blood, pain and bruises, the baby...it was all getting to be too much. She just couldn't take any more. She was going to do what she wanted and how she wanted to do it. She was exhausted, in pain, and she wanted out of here, *with* Jerry.

Tommy and Emil looked at each other in shock at her outburst. Shaking his head, Emil moved on to make room for the cart.

The only thing that made it feasible was the fact there was less debris that had to be moved to roll the cart through or around. At least she would have his body to bury, not left in some destroyed cement grave. It was little comfort, but she was grabbing at what she could get.

It took almost an hour, moving slowly, to find a staircase that was passable. When one was found, Emil went first, and Larry followed, helping him clear debris. The two of them seemed to have become good friends. Grace was so grateful for that. She figured the two of them would need each other when they got out of this mess.

Tommy and Jawad maneuvered the cart down the stairs. With Jerry on board, it was heavy and slow going. Grace was told to follow behind in case she fell, and then she would fall into Jawad, who laughed and nodded his agreement when Tommy explained it to her.

Step by step, pain by pain, the group made it down the stairway until the door to the garage was facing them!

CHAPTER

TWENTY-ONE

Things weren't getting any better inside the building for Grace, and Tag wanted to get her out of there more than ever. He could hear in her voice she was scared and something else... he couldn't put his finger on it, but something more was wrong.

It was still nagging at him when he came out from hiding behind the SUV.

He had to find a way to get inside and save his wife.

(((**Boom**)))

Startled, Tag swung around to face the blast. It sounded like it had come from the section of the building Grace said they were in. Oh, *dear God, dear God! No...no...NO...!*

He turned, and there were more reporters closing in on him.

"Mr. Reynolds...Mr. Reynolds."

Tag took off running in the opposite direction. He seriously needed to get away from the reporters before he could even attempt to get into the building. He turned a corner and realized he was back at the command center.

The group of FBI men who were standing along the perimeter would certainly keep the media away from him.

When he stepped up to the barricade, he noticed the man he had spoken to earlier when they were using the drone. Tag waved his hand, and the man came over.

"I have information you might want to hear." Tag was desperate now. His wife was not going to last much longer, if she was still alive.

"We saw you on the news. That was stupid talking to the reporter. The FBI guys are angry." The man turned and started to walk away.

"You don't understand. I know the type of bomb, which means I understand what type of person will do this." He pushed against the guards.

"I'm sorry, but I don't think we need your help right now. We have things happening."

Really? Like what? You aren't DOING anything but waiting for my wife to blow up!

"But, I'm speaking to my wife on the phone." The man continued to walk away from him, and Tag pushed harder against the guards and yelled, "You need to get the people out of there."

This time the guards weren't just standing as he pushed against them. One of them pushed him back, which sent Tag's instinct into high alert. Before he could think about it, he slammed his fist into one guard's chin, making contact.

The guards didn't need another punch before they started to reciprocate. Fists were flying as Tag continued to get through them. All the time, the media was filming the whole scene.

Tag had to be pulled off of them.

"Okay, Mr. Reynolds. Since you are a veteran, serving our country during this terrible time of war and due to your press entourage" — the FBI agent pointed to the cameras and reporters lining the barricade right in front of where they had taken Tag after the fight — "...we have decided to let you go. But we insist that you leave the area. We understand you want to help so you can be reunited with your wife, but you need to let us do our jobs."

Tag rubbed his wrists where the handcuffs had been tightly placed when they locked him to a chair. Now he was being told to leave the area. He knew there wasn't any possible way for him to do that. And they must have been stupid to think he would.

"Would it be at least possible for me to help the firefighters and other rescue workers in clearing out the rubble? This way it is one more hand helping to get my wife out of there. And, Lord knows I need something else to think about."

The FBI agent thought about it for a little while, even going to check with another member of the team. When he came back, he had a frown on his face.

"As long as you promise to only help with the rubble, it would be nice having another hand. Plus it would be good for the news to see you helping to get your wife out instead of fighting with the people trying to do the same."

Tag smiled, although inside he was steaming. Another fight wouldn't help the matter, and taking a swing at the FBI agent would only get him handcuffed and probably taken straight to jail.

Who are they kidding? I am the only one trying to get my wife out. No one else is! God — please help me!

Helping to remove the rubble from the entrance would place him within earshot of the command tent. If something happened or something was about to happen, he would be able to pick up on the commotion. If worse came to worse, he would be able to call Grace and give her a heads-up. If Grace was still okay.

The FBI agents left him alone, and Tag looked around the area once more from his prison chair. He had noticed they weren't making any progress in determining if it was safe to enter or not, while he sat handcuffed to a stupid chair. *The chances of their getting inside the building before nightfall were looking less likely by the minute. It was pushing six o'clock now.*

Once night hit, it would be harder and harder for them to determine the safety of the building. Time was starting to become an issue, along with wondering if another bomb would go off at any minute.

How many had it been? Eight...no, nine. Nine bombs had gone off. If the feds were right about the note, there could be one more. He wouldn't allow himself to think about that now.

Once un-cuffed, Tag jumped up from the chair and grabbed one of the fluorescent vests to head out of the tent. The media was instantly aware of him. The reporters started to yell questions, while the cameramen moved around in the hopes of getting the perfect shot.

He gave them a little wave, not wanting to deal with any of their questions at the moment. He turned and headed into the disaster zone in hopes of at least helping to get a piece of the front entrance cleared.

~ ~ ~

Tag had told Grace once they reached the parking garage, they would be able to climb out of the building through the opening the drone had used to enter. All they needed to do was reach the parking garage. Once there, it was only a matter of finding the drone and then getting out.

Another contraction hit Grace, this time causing her to bend over. Everyone stopped while Tommy came rushing to her side.

"Maybe this isn't a good idea."

"Yes it is. We need to get to the parking garage." Her words were pushed out with a deep breath.

Tommy had come to recognize during their adventure through the building the breathing she used to help when a contraction came. Now he stood beside her, encouraging her to breathe in and out.

Tommy joined in, realizing that it helped him feel better, too. Once the pain settled down, he went back to rolling Jerry. But he continued to talk to her and the others.

Then they heard it. Another bomb went off. It seemed to be somewhere above them, but Grace couldn't pinpoint it. The building shook, and more debris fell. Everyone stopped, waiting for the building to stop shaking, and then just went on moving forward.

Grace was amazed. *Could we really be getting used to being bombed? Explosion, move on. Explosion, move on...*

"Have you been timing how far those pains are apart? Isn't that something you are supposed to do?" It was Emil who brought her out of her thoughts.

"They haven't reached that point yet."

"Okay. I just wanted to make sure that you weren't going to be suddenly screaming that you could feel the head."

Grace laughed, although she realized from the look on Emil's face that he wasn't joking around. He continued, "I think I have it cleared enough to get through the garage door! See what you guys think. If the cart will make it through, Grace will be able to make it."

They could see emergency lights coming from the garage, which was a relief. Some were broken from the ceiling falling, but most of them still existed.

Emil went through first and they maneuvered Jerry and the cart through. It must have taken a good fifteen minutes to make it happen.

Everyone gave a sigh of relief when it was over. Jawad went through next, and Tommy stayed to help Grace get through the opening.

"Ready?" Tommy was more worried than she was.

She nodded her head and knew in her heart there wasn't any alternative. She *had* to be ready. The sharp edges might be a little rough, but she was going to get through the piles of concrete and plaster one way or another. Grace wanted out of this building, and every contraction she had pushed her that much more to make it happen.

It was very uncomfortable, even painful at times, but Grace slowly came out on the other side. When she was able to stand, she saw there were only a few more bloody scratches.

It was then the baby gave her a large kick, warping her stomach for all the guys to see. At first they were shocked; then, realizing she made it and the baby was healthy, all three of the guys laughed and congratulated each other. Even Larry smiled.

Emil even gave Grace a hug. Larry started to hug her but then felt awkward and just shook her hand instead. Grace felt like she had just won an Olympic medal! She gave them all a great big smile.

"Have you ever seen such a beautiful pregnant woman in your life?" It was Tommy who was the most proud of her.

The guys all agreed, and Grace could feel the heat in her cheeks.

Then Tommy wrapped his arms around her shoulder and practically dragged her to an area that looked like it had the least destruction, even though small pieces of concrete continued to fall. He then moved Jerry and the cart next to her.

They had made it to the parking garage. Once she was able to sit down, her discomfort started to subside.

"That wasn't a normal contraction, was it?" Tommy kicked small pieces of debris out of the way as he moved the cart over to her.

"No. That was something else."

"And we both know what 'else' it was. We have to get you out of here." Tommy started to look around. Once he knew that she was feeling better, he got up and started to walk around. He was looking for some way out. If he didn't find the drone, he could at least find some opening in the shattered foundation.

Emil also went exploring. He said he would scream until he didn't have a voice left, if it meant getting someone in there to get them out.

All of the guys slowly walked the area, stepping over or moving debris. Every little item was examined to see if it was important. For approximately ten minutes, no one said a word.

After Emil had moved several yards away, he stepped on something that crunched. He looked down to discover a smashed helicopter-type thing lying on the ground. He took a few more steps and wasn't expecting what he found.

"Um... Tommy... You guys...You need to come over here!"

When Emil yelled for Tommy, Grace's hopes jumped. She rose slowly and lumbered her way to where Tommy was catching up to Emil. Jawad was right behind her, with Larry being the last to arrive.

Looking down at the drone Emil had stepped on, Tommy smiled, "Hey! Good news!" Jawad and Larry yelled and cheered at the discovery. Everyone, except Emil, was smiling.

Emil wasn't looking at the drone on the ground at all. He was looking up and quietly said, "Not that. *THAT!*"

Everyone looked up where he was staring, and directly in front of them, they saw their worst nightmare.

Wrapped around a huge column that looked like it was a major support of the garage was a bomb. And attached to the bomb was a digital timer, which was slowly counting down. They were closer to zero than Grace would have liked — less than twenty minutes.

Dear God, how much more can we take?

It was will power alone that kept Grace from passing out.

CHAPTER

TWENTY-TWO

The entire world was watching as Tag pulled one piece of shattered concrete after another from the entrance to the building. Even the reporters were quiet. No one said a word. Nobody.

The world was quietly focused on the man who was trying to do anything he could to get to his wife and unborn child.

Although there were a lot of people around him helping to remove broken pieces of the building, he had never felt so alone. He knew that his life had changed that morning when the first bombs went off. And it would never be the same again.

His drinking days were over; he knew that now, along with feeling sorry for himself. When he got Grace back in his arms, he was going to do everything in his power to make the past few months up to her. He even thought about them renewing their wedding vows — after his son was born, of course.

A nagging thought hit him that maybe she wouldn't make it out, that the baby would be born inside that disaster, or worse, the baby would die inside this carnage.

Terrified, he pushed the ugly thoughts away. He had to keep thinking positively. The negative thoughts needed to be in the past if he was going to get through this and make sure his wife and child got out of this situation in one piece.

His phone went off, and he nearly jumped out of his skin.

"Grace?"

"Tag! We made it... the parking garage... you said.... Problem... we... another bomb. It's... a column."

Tag's heart stopped at that moment. His wife and child were standing in the vicinity of another bomb that could go off at any time. Another bomb. That would be number ten.

He took a deep breath and pulled his training to the front of his mind. He couldn't focus on the danger right now.

He needed to help her to get through this.

"Can you see any way out from where you are? Any light coming in from the outside?"

"No, none that...can see. Some emergency lights are...we have...go by."

"Okay." He knew what he was going to have to do, and he didn't like it one bit, but this was the only way he would be able to save his wife. He looked around at all the cameras.

Doing this on national television wasn't what he wanted, but maybe the FBI would take the situation a little more seriously if it was shown on TV. But, then again, would they? He wasn't even sure he cared what they did any more. For the last several hours, they had done nothing but watch.

The phone connection to Grace was sketchy, but he understood the majority of what she was telling him. She was telling him that the timer was saying they had less than twenty minutes to get this thing done.

Trying not to panic himself or anyone around him, he calmly turned toward the people who were digging beside him.

"Let's move to the other side of this garage area. There are people there who need to get out." He couldn't tell them that a bomb was going to go off soon. Not only would they not help him, but they would run away themselves.

He knew he had to get the people to the other side of the garage, as far away from the bomb as they could get. Tag and the other volunteers would then have to dig them out from there.

But there was something that had to be done first.

"Grace, there is something I need you to do for me."

The people around him looked confused at what he was saying to his wife.

Addressing the crew again, he said, "They are on the other side of that wall." He pointed to the area that was opposite the parking garage where the drone had entered.

"We need to make the area bigger so they can get out." He then turned back to his wife on the phone.

CHAPTER

TWENTY-THREE

"There is something I need you to do." Those words from Tag sent a shiver through Grace's body. She stepped even closer to the bomb, and Tommy put a hand on her shoulder. She pressed the speaker button on her phone and handed it to him to hold.

"I put you on speaker. Tommy is holding the phone. He's been helping me this whole time. He is a great guy. My other friends here are Emil, Larry, and Jawad." She looked at her companions, and they took turns saying hello to Tag.

"You need to look at the device and tell me exactly what you see — every little detail — so I can get a mental image of what we are dealing with." Tag's voice coming through the speaker gave Grace the confidence she needed to step right up to the bomb, which was looming right in front of her.

"There are ten metal tubes with green wires coming out of the top. The metal is black and reminds me of a dumbbell. The wires run together right above the time display, with five different wires coming out and into the area behind the clock.

"Tag, the clock section reminds me of some type of computer circuit board — but different. The timer shows only sixteen minutes left."

"Stay calm, honey. Dig in your purse. Do you still keep your nail clippers in there?"

Grace turned and grabbed the purse she had set on the ground when Tag had initially asked her to look at the bomb. She started to rummage through it, hoping that when she'd changed to this purse, she hadn't ignored the clippers. When she found them, she pulled them out and held them up. "I got them."

"Okay, this is what I will need you do...."

"What are you doing?" Suddenly frightened that she was going to set off the bomb, Jawad stepped up to Grace and Tommy, causing Grace to give a start and drop the clippers.

Emil grabbed Jawad by the back of the neck while Tommy reared back, holding his fist ready to land a punch on Jawad.

Larry screamed, "I knew it was him!"

"What are you trying to do? Blow us up? You can't just go pulling wires off that thing!" Jawad seemed terrified.

Grace realized they thought Jawad was a threat and stepped between them

"Stop!" She placed a hand on Tommy's chest. "Jawad isn't the bad guy here. I figured out who is, and it isn't him."

Everyone stopped and stared at her!

"What? You know who set off all of these bombs?" Tommy still didn't want to let Jawad out of his sight.

"Of course, she does," said a soft, sweet voice. "She's a smart woman, what with all her questions." Fred Mason stepped out from behind the column, using a long stick for a cane. He looked half dead himself.

"I figured this was where you were headed, after the last bomb revealed that you had left that area. Having a bomb-squad hubby. Smart, too. It's the obvious place for the last one. It will take down whatever is left standing."

He went on, "So, Grace, when did you figure out it was me?"

Everyone turned to stare at her. "Every time a bomb went off, you said, 'I can't believe it didn't kill me,' or something to that effect. Everyone else was grateful that they weren't killed. After a while, it became obvious to me: You *wanted* to die and was having a hard time getting it done.

"I thought you had finally gotten your wish when you appeared to be dead. Guess that one didn't work for you, either. This was your grand suicide event, wasn't it?"

"I prefer to think of is as my Grand Exit, not suicide. When I awoke lying in that room where you'd left me, I was so disappointed. What is the problem here? Why can't I die? Everyone else was dying!

"Yeah, I was afraid I had let myself talk too much. Couldn't understand why I didn't die on that first round. I was certainly close enough. And then the sec...."

"Listen, Fred. It doesn't have to be like this. We can all get out, and it will be over." Grace was desperate at this point.

"Yes, I'm afraid it *does* have to be like this, Grace. Now move away from the bomb. I had hoped you and your baby would get out of this, but I can see that you are the one I should have been worried about from the start."

He pulled out a gun and stressed his point by aiming it straight at Grace's head. He took her cell phone out of Tommy's hand and smashed it on the ground. Grace looked at her lifeline to her husband disappear. In fact, she could see her entire life coming to an end.

~~~

When an unknown voice joined Grace's and the other guys', Tag knew there was trouble. He heard Grace being threatened, and then her phone went dead. He threw his own phone to the ground and frantically started to dig.

During his conversation with Grace, he had made his way opposite the area where the drone had gone through. Now his only hope of helping his wife was to dig her out.

Come on, Grace! Get to the far wall! Now!

About two seconds later, the bomb exploded!

The entire structure shook and threw the workers backwards to the ground. The building grumbled and swayed like it was taking its last breath. To the workers, being so close to the source of the explosion, the noise was deafening.

Tag's heart stopped. *Why did the bomb go off early?*

He knew. He knew his family was gone, but he had to find them. He wouldn't stop until they were out of there. He couldn't think of anything else. Not now.

With tears flowing, he used everything he had to start digging. He pulled boulders out, not even noticing their weight or the cuts they caused on his hands.

When a hand reached beside him, he realized that others had joined him; together, they pulled and dug. When his hand finally went through the opening, he knew he was close. He dug faster until he had a hole big enough for his body.

Without even thinking, he leaned into the hole and then wiggled until he got his entire body through. People were yelling and screaming on the outside for him to get out, but he didn't care. He wasn't concerned about the danger or the anger of the authorities.

Let them arrest me when I come out with my wife. That was all that mattered — getting Grace out of this building. He braced himself for what he would find.

The area was dark. No more emergency lights. It took him a moment to get his eyes adjusted. The only flashlight he had was a small one he kept in his pocket, but at this point, anything was better than nothing. He remembered seeing this far-off area when the drone had first gone in. It had turned left and then went straight.

Slowly and quietly, remembering his days over in Iraq when he had to secretly enter a building to stop a terrorist, he began to search for his wife.

He checked out the structure as he made his way along the wall. The only sound was the groaning of the crumbling cement structure. It was obvious the building wasn't going to stand much longer.

Clinging close to the walls, he almost stumbled over something. He flashed the little light down and found that it was a man and someone else — Grace! Her head was lying in the man's lap!

He'd found her. He'd found GRACE!

Neither one of them was responsive. In his attempt to get around to Grace, he hit a cart with a body on it. He barely glanced at it in the near dark. Grace was all that mattered.

Tag swept Grace up in his arms and started back for the hole. He could feel debris sticking out of her back, oozing blood. He were no signs of life, but that wasn't going to stop him from getting her out of this living hell.

When he appeared with a pregnant woman in his arms, loud cheers came from everywhere. Tag didn't feel the joy. He knew she hadn't survived that last blast. He knew, and it was killing him.

Volunteers took her and got her into an ambulance that quickly drove away, with sirens screaming.

Tag's heart was breaking as he watched the ambulance leave with Grace in the back. Then he turned back for the other two men. He didn't think they would be alive either, but if he could reach them, they weren't going to stay in this hole.

Leave no man behind? Okay, but only if he could keep his thoughts off of his wife. The pain was almost more than he could bear.

Tag found that the man had fallen over on the ground after he'd removed Grace. He pulled him up onto his feet, and that's when he realized that the guy was just a kid. Well, he seemed like a kid to him. He couldn't be more than, what — nineteen? Twenty? Tag was shocked to hear a groan come from him. *He's alive!*

Tag rushed as fast as he could to get him back to the outside opening. When the volunteers started pulling the man through. Tag yelled at them that he was still alive! There was more cheering.

Again, from just inside the hole, Tag watched as the man was put into an ambulance and taken away.

There was one last thing he had to do. Tag told the helpers that there was one more to come out. Just as he turned to go back down, a large part of the garage area came crashing down. It took several minutes before the dust settled enough for him to see again with his small light.

Everyone was begging him to come out. It was too dangerous to go back after that last person, who was probably already dead. Tag actually thought about it for a moment, but like any Marine, he was not going to leave the man if he could find him.

He turned back to the darkness and had a hard time finding his way back to the same area as before. It had fallen in. Walls were broken; large cement stones were in new places.

The little light wasn't helping much. He tripped over a rock of some kind and went sprawling in the opposite direction.

Tag lay on the floor for a moment waiting for the pain to subside. He didn't know how much more he could take before he fell apart emotionally. He had hurt his back and shoulder, but he had to keep going.

As he was trying to get up, he felt the cart near his right leg. The collapsing building had sent it rolling away from where it had been. He quickly got to his feet to feel if the man was still on the slab. He was, but Tag knew the cart was not going to roll back to the hole to get him out.

There was only one option left. Tag picked him up and put him over the shoulder that had not been injured. Even though he felt no life in him, Tag went back toward the safety of the daylight coming through the hole.

It was when he went to hand off the man to the helpers that he noticed who he was dealing with. Jerry! *Jerry?* How did Jerry get here? Tag was more than stunned; he almost passed out from the shock.

Jerry was quickly removed by ambulance. Tag slid back down into the hole. He had to be alone. He buried his head in his hands and cried. Near hysterics, he drained his heart in that bombed-out building.

Sobbing was the only way he could deal with the pain in his heart. It had probably been not more than five minutes or so, but Tag felt he had been there for hours. When he could control his emotions again, he crawled back up the stones to the opening.

Tag stepped out of the ruins of what used to be a thriving post office. The news media and crowd were cheering him and clapping.

It was obvious they didn't see the tears running down his dirty face. He had lost his wife, his son, and his best friend, all in one day.

He was going into shock when they put him in the remaining ambulance and drove him away.

The structure behind him imploded like a sinkhole.

CHAPTER

TWENTY-FOUR

Grace awoke in an Intensive Care Unit. At first she didn't know where she was or why. One thing that made her happy was to see Tag by her bed. He was kissing her hand and talking to her, although she had no idea what he was saying.

She started to move, and it startled Tag. He yelled for the nurses and doctors and anyone else who would listen. Her head was pounding. When she reached for it, a nurse grabbed her hand and told her to leave it alone.

"You have a concussion, Grace, numerous cuts and abrasions, and certainly your share of bruises, but you are going to be all right." The name tag she was wearing said "Nurse Kathy."

"Thank you," she replied in a voice that was barely more than a whisper. Medication was wearing on her, too, so she fell back to sleep.

During the next two days, Grace had piecemeal memories of people in her room, coming and going, but nothing made sense. She didn't even care. She just wanted to rest.

Police officers were sitting by her bed at one point — at least that's what she thought they were. A man she thought was holding a puppy in a blanket was standing by the window once. Some doctor by the name of "memberme" kept showing up.

It was about noon on the third day that she woke up fairly clear-headed and aware of her surroundings. When she opened her eyes, she saw Tag sleeping in a chair by her bed. She was in a private room, which worried her because she knew they couldn't afford it.

It was time to return to her nightmare and put the pieces together. She knew in her heart she had lost her little baby in that last blast. Grace was amazed that *she* had even survived.

"Tag..." She was shocked to see bruises on his face. He looked as if he had been in a fight of some kind.

Tag jumped up from the chair and ran to her bedside. He bent down and kissed her all over her face and hugged her. He was crying, and that made her cry.

"I love you, I love you, I love you! I will never let another day go by without telling you that!" Tag was choking on his own tears.

"Love me? After I got our baby killed? How could you possibly love me?" Grace was in so much pain over the effects of just one day. The loss of the child she wanted so badly would be with her for the rest of her life. Her tears told of the pain in her heart.

"Grace, I will be right back. Don't go anywhere, I will be right back!" Tag ran for the door.

"Where would I....." Grace sighed and laid her head back down, the tears still falling.

About two minutes later, Tag came walking in with a baby wrapped up in a tiny blanket. Grace's eyes became huge. Was this what she thought it was?

"Is that him? Is that our son!?" Grace was now almost yelling.

"Uh, no, Grace. I'm so sorry. This is *not* our son, honey — this is our *daughter!*" Tag was so proud he could hardly contain himself.

He put the baby in her mother's arms, and they both cried. She undid the blanket and the clothes just to make sure she was all there, and, sure enough, the baby was perfect. Her little face was the perfect combination of her parents' features.

"No problems whatsoever! She is perfect. You did awesome, Mom! 'Course, it was by C-section since you wanted to sleep through it all..." Tag kissed them both.

The love for her little girl never left her face, but the happiness did as police officers walked into her room. She knew she would have to relive it all, so she might as well get it over with.

"Mrs. Reynolds, how nice to see you recovering. And congratulations on the beautiful little girl. I am Detective Ben Harrison, and this is my partner, Detective Jon Dartmore. Right now we just need to know what happened in that garage after your phone went dead. Your husband got us to that part. The early part of the day, we can deal with after you have recovered a little more."

Grace took a moment to put all of her thoughts in order and then started.

"I was down there with Tommy, Jawad, Emil, this teenager named Larry, and Jerry. We thought Fred Mason had died in one of the last blasts, so we left him, and the others, where they'd fallen.

"It took a long while to get to the basement, but when we did, we discovered a bomb attached to what appeared to be the main pillar. I was talking with Tag about it when he said he wanted me to describe it to him. I knew he was going to try to get me to disengage it. I was terrified at the thought.

"Anyway, just as I was letting my husband know what it looked like and how it was put together, Fred Mason came suddenly into view. He pulled a gun and pointed it at my head. That's when he shattered my phone. We all argued with him, wanting to know why, etc.

"He said he'd been married to the love of his life for forty-eight years and that she'd died two years ago. They had no children. Less than a year later, due to all the cutbacks and his age, he was laid off from his job there at the post office.

"They had taken the only thing he had left to live for. His broken heart was stepped on, and he couldn't deal with it. Fred said he wanted to make sure no one else ever worked there again.

"Emil argued that we were innocent people and had done nothing to him — so why was he trying to kill us? Fred said he just didn't care about anything or anyone anymore. His life was over, so why not ours, too? He said he had ten bombs set up to go off at different times, set to take the whole post office down; however, he had expected to die when the first one went off.

"When he didn't, he tried to be where the next one was going to go off so that he could die then. When that didn't happen, he kept moving and so on.

"He said that, when we thought he was dead, he was only unconscious. Near death, but only unconscious. When he came to, Fred said he was so angry to still be alive. He decided to take it out on us and arranged for the ninth bomb to go off where we said we were going, but we had already left to find a way to the parking garage. Tag's insistence that we get to the garage saved us from dying in that blast."

Grace smiled and looked at her husband with such love that it embarrassed the detectives.

"Since Fred was still alive and there was only one bomb left, he made his way down to the parking garage, and that's when he found us getting ready to disarm it. Fred said he couldn't allow that to happen. He planned on being right next to the bomb this time to make sure he died." Grace was near tears with her thoughts. Tag held her hand.

"Mrs. Reynolds, the bomb in the garage went off more than ten minutes before it was supposed to. Can you tell us why?" It was Detective Harrison again.

"Yes. We watched him all the time. When he wasn't looking at us, Emil nodded his head for Tommy to take me and Larry to the far wall, back where I was before, as soon as he gave him the word. Jawad was also watching the signals and agreed with them. I remember that nice man smiled and winked at me. I am pretty sure Jawad was aware of the danger, but he didn't flinch.

"Fred said there was no need to wait for the bomb to go off; all he had to do was move the clock hands around and let it explode now. When Fred turned toward the column to alter the timing device on the bomb, Emil nodded to Tommy, who grabbed me and ran for the far wall. Larry refused to come with me. I heard him screaming about Fred killing his mother.

"The guys jumped Fred, and they yelled that he wasn't going to kill any more people today. That's when the explosion happened.

"I felt intense pain in my back, like I had been shot several times, and then I blacked out. When I came to, Tommy was leaning against the wall, unconscious. We had made it to the opposite wall, but it didn't seem to do much good. We were in pretty bad shape.

"I knew in my heart I was going to die there, so I crawled up closer to

Tommy and laid my head on his lap. That's the last I remember."

The detectives asked a couple more questions, wrote down everything, and then stood up.

"Thank you, Mrs. Reynolds. I know I speak for my whole department when I say you are one brave lady. And we have to admit, your husband wasn't too bad, either. A royal pain in the neck, mind you, but an okay guy." After the chuckles stopped, the detectives said their goodbyes.

After the detectives left, Tag and Grace spent the afternoon just looking into each other's eyes or at their baby. Tag was the first to say it.

"I'm so sorry..."

"No, don't be. I am the one..."

"What kind of husband would...?"

"I didn't know what you were..."

It became obvious there wasn't anything more to say. They had their love for each other, and, right now, that was all that mattered.

"While you had nothing better to do than sleep, I put together all the baby furniture at home and have it all in place. There is even a picture of her beautiful mother sitting on the dresser."

"Nothing better to....!" She punched his arm, and he pretended it was painful.

"So, does it look nice? The furniture, I mean?"

"Yep. Sure does. But not as nice as when she gets to sleep there."

Though Grace's heart was full of love and thankfulness for her baby's and her own health, she turned serious.

"Tag, I have to know. Tell me about everyone. I have to know the truth." Grace clenched her teeth for just a moment, fighting back the oncoming tears. Then she looked up, ready to hear whatever he had to say.

Tag hung his head most of the time he talked, but sometimes he would look up to see her response.

"Your friend Tommy didn't make it, Grace. He just had too many injuries. He was still alive when I got him out, but they told me he died on the way to the hospital.

"The two guys who jumped Fred — uh, Emil and Jawad? — they died with Fred when the bomb went off. The kid, Larry, was right beside them and died as well. That tenth blast was connected to the last strong support left in the building. After I got you out, the building completely caved in. They are supposed to start clearing the area and searching for bodies tomorrow or the next day. They expect to find quite a few."

Grace had one last comment. "We lost Jerry." It wasn't a question. She already knew the answer. She was dreading what Tag would think of her for getting his best friend killed.

"Oh...Jerry. Do you mean the Jerry that drove you to the post office? *THAT* Jerry?" Tag looked up and smiled! "He will be just fine! You saved his life, Grace! He has a bum leg, but he is just as happy as ever!"

"Oh, I'm so sorry, Tag — wait: *WHAT?* No way! Jerry? *Our* Jerry? No way!" Grace was having a hard time digesting the information. "I don't believe you. I can't believe...are you sure?"

Grace couldn't get past the fact that Jerry had actually made it. All the times she'd looked at his "dead body," he was actually alive! *How about that? Jerry is alive! Wow!*

"Where is he? When can I see him?" Grace was beside herself. She was so sure he was dead all the time that she was pushing that cart, but she just couldn't leave him behind.

"He will be here in a couple of hours or so. He said to tell, uh, 'the most beautiful woman in the world' that he loved her and owed her his life. Which he does, of course!" Tag was laughing but was so proud of Grace for not leaving their best friend behind.

"I can't wait." Grace was crying, but this time it was out of pure joy.

"Tag, one last thing. I want to pick the name for our little girl." Grace was tenderly holding her baby up to her face.

"Anything you want, darling. I knew you would want to, so I never gave it a thought. I will love any name you want for her." It was obvious from the look on his face that Tag meant it.

"Mr. Reynolds, I would like to present to you, Miss Tommie Lee Reynolds."

CHAPTER

TWENTY-FIVE

"This is Marion Anderson, coming to you from the site of the former post office which was bombed less than a week ago. Most of you know the story of what happened and the 154 people who tragically died here. You have also been informed of the incredible rescue of Grace Reynolds by her husband, Tag Reynolds. Grace, who was nine months pregnant, gave birth to a healthy baby girl.

"Well I am here to tell you some of the good news that has come out of this terrible tragedy. During this horrific time for Mrs. Reynolds, a young student, Tommy Lee Walters, took it upon himself to protect her from the destructive ravages all around. Unfortunately, Mr. Walters died in his last attempt to save his new friend, Grace.

"Mr. Walters was at the post office to mail his scholarship papers for the coming school year. He was a fashion student at University of North Texas. We have been informed this morning that the University has set up a one-million-dollar Tommy Lee Walters Scholarship Fund for promising fashion students. Though his career and life were cut short, I believe he would be smiling at this new development.

"I would further like to add that Tag and Grace Reynolds have named their new daughter 'Tommie Lee,' after the brave young man who constantly protected Grace and her baby.

"Mr. Tag Reynolds, who has become a huge celebrity across this nation for his incredible bravery, has been offered many career opportunities throughout the United States. We could not reach Mr. Reynolds for a comment, as we are told he is in seclusion with his wife and new baby.

"Mrs. Reynolds has been offered a book deal as well as a contract for the film rights to her story of surviving this tragedy.

"The only other survivor of the bombing is alive due only to the heroics of Grace Reynolds herself. Everyone thought Jerry Barker was dead, but she refused to let him go. She had him rolled around on a cart the entire time, protecting him to the end.

"We are told he will have a limp from damage to his hip and leg, but he told us that will just make him more sympathetic to the ladies. However, Stephanie, his new fiancée, stepped in at that moment and warned any 'sympathetic' ladies to stay away.

"Mr. Jerry Barker is finishing his degree in a few months, and his father has announced he plans to retire and turn the company over to his son to run.

"I am sure you are very well aware of the company we are speaking of Barker and Son Builders, the multi-million-dollar construction company. Very few areas of Dallas/Ft. Worth can say there isn't one of their buildings close by!

"In addition, the Internal Revenue Service has announced it has issued a six-month extension for any Dallas residents whose tax returns were late or destroyed in the fires.

"Last but not least, the burned-out rubble you see behind me is only temporary. The U.S. government and the State of Texas announced this morning that they will be replacing this old building with a post office that will take technology into the future. The opening is expected in approximately three years.

"So, there you have it. While the city, state, and even our country mourns those whose lives have been lost, we wanted you to know some good can come out of bad. This is Marion Anderson. Back to the news-room."

EPILOGUE

Due to all of the publicity, Grace's parents saw everything that had happened, and changed their minds about the status of their son-in-law. They contacted her, asking for a reunion. Because Tag was all for it, Grace consented.

The damage to Jerry's leg caused him to walk with a limp for the rest of his life and sometimes required the use of a cane. All other injuries healed properly. A few months later, Jerry graduated college and married his fiancé, Stephanie. Tag and Grace were the Best Man and Matron of Honor at the ceremony.

Tommie Lee Reynolds was ring bearer, even though she was only five months old at the time. Jerry's father, Mason Barker, proudly walked down the aisle carrying her while she held the rings. At her birth, he declared to the world she was his first grandchild.

Tag and Grace had to beg Jerry's parents to stop buying Tommie so many gifts. They were pretty sure their little girl was set for life!

A year later, Stephanie gave birth to identical twin boys whom they named Jason Daniel and Jeremy Damon. They were the spitting image of their father. Whenever their mother wanted them, she would call "J.D.!" and both would come running.

Four months after the birth of Jerry and Stephanie's twins, Grace gave birth to another baby girl they named Melinda Grace, who was her mother all over again.

Jerry took over his father's business. Mason and his wife, Ellen, took off in their new RV to enjoy retirement, but were always home to celebrate holidays and birthdays with their grandchildren.

The elderly Barker's made it clear they had always looked at Tag as another son, therefore his family was always a part of that group. Grace's parents came to visit about two times a year, but their lives were so wrapped around their own friends in California that they couldn't stay long.

Tag was true to his word and never touched alcohol again. He went regularly to PTSD meetings with Jerry until they both felt they had their feet back on the ground. Tag works as Jerry's General Foreman in the construction business.

With their deep friendship and long history together, they made a business dynamic that doubled the size of the already successful company, within five years.

The two couples purchased large homes next door to each other and spend all their free time together cooking out and swimming in one of their pools, while their children played together. The fence was removed between their two backyards making one large playground for the children and their puppies.

Grace never returned to her job with the magazine. After her recovery, she became a stay-at-home mom who writes mystery novels that have consistently hit the best seller lists.

Her first book, *"Surviving On The Inside,"* was the true story of her being trapped in the post office. Before it even hit the book shelves, there was a movie deal in the works. There has been speculation that the beautiful Mrs. Reynolds may even play herself.

When Tommie Lee was five years old and Melinda Grace was four, Grace gave birth to a son they named Carson Dwayne.

But his mother calls him 'Taglet.'

~~~~~~~~~~~~~~~~~~~

I sincerely hope you enjoyed this book. If you did, please take just a moment to leave a review at Amazon.com

Thank you and God Bless.

Donalie